Hippie Chick

Hippie Chick

Joseph Monninger

FRONT STREET
Asheville, North Carolina

For Wendy and Justin, who told me
about manatees a long time ago
—J.M.

Printed in the United States of America
Designed by Helen Robinson
First edition

Library of Congress Cataloging-in-Publication Data
Monninger, Joseph.
Hippie chick / Joseph Monninger.—1st ed.
p. cm.
Summary: After her sailboat capsizes, fifteen-year-old
Lolly Emmerson is rescued by manatees and taken to a
mangrove key in the Everglades, where she forms a bond
with her aquatic companions while struggling to survive.
ISBN 978-1-59078-598-0 (hardcover : alk. paper)
[1. Survival—Fiction. 2. Manatees—Fiction.
3. Mangrove swamps—Fiction.
4. Shipwrecks—Fiction. 5. Sailing—Fiction.
6. Everglades (Fla.)—Fiction.] I. Title.
PZ7.M7537Hip 2008
[Fic]—dc22
2007051976

FRONT STREET
An Imprint of Boyds Mills Press, Inc.
815 Church Street
Honesdale, Pennsylvania 18431

Hippie Chick

I am the magical mouse
I don't eat cheese
I eat sunsets
And the tops of trees

—*Kenneth Patchen,*
from "The Magical Mouse"

1

The day it happened: November 17, a Friday
Temperature: 82 degrees
Wind: SW 7 knots
Moon stage: Full, or nearly
High tide: 4:37 p.m.

Here's the thing: if Nicky had kept kissing me, this wouldn't have happened. None of it. Because as long as Nicky wanted to kiss me, I wanted to kiss him, and we kissed for around an hour, I swear, him sitting on the gunwale of my boat, his legs spread, and me in between his legs, and he smelled like sun and baby lotion and the ocean. He's twenty, I'm fifteen. Some local people think that Nicky probably shouldn't be making out with a fifteen-year-old and so we try not to hang all over each other in public. In fact, I wouldn't have been making out with him at all if the Donaldsons had been home, but I knew they weren't. They had gone shopping for the weekend groceries, and Mrs. Donaldson, known to everyone as Sammy, had called to me before they left to see if I needed anything. But I didn't. I had stocked up on my way over to the *Mugwump*—

it's less than a mile from my house—and said thanks, no problem, and she stood for a second looking down at me, her hand up to cover her eyes. I love Mrs. Donaldson; she's kind of like watching a 1950s TV show. She is a friend of my mom's and is a bit square and a bit conventional, but she lets me moor my boat at her dock, and she looks out for me, and she knocks herself out trying to match every outfit she puts on. I *know* it pains her to see how I dress, and once or twice she had said something, but nothing in a mean way. She has brought me sweaters and things from someone's sister or cousin, and she leaves them folded on the deck near the boat.

Anyway, she stood for a second with one hip out, her hand up to shade her eyes, and smiled at me. Her lipstick gleamed in the late afternoon sun.

"I'm meeting Joe at the Surfside," she said, mentioning a restaurant she liked to visit with her husband, "but I shouldn't be back late. Are you sure you don't need anything?"

"Positive," I said. "Thanks."

"Are you sailing tonight?"

"Full moon," I said. "I might."

"Well, leave a note if you go. And please don't be out too long."

I promised. I wasn't even sure I wanted to sail, but it was a beautiful night and I thought I might take the boat out. I had various runs that took me different distances. I could do a short loop in about an hour and I knew all the landmarks dead cold. I had already checked the weather, which promised to be clear and comfortable, with a slight chop of a foot or two. I decided, though, not to make a decision.

Then Mrs. Donaldson pulled out and Nicky pulled in.

"Hey," he said.

He parked his bike against a dock railing and climbed into the boat. He wore a pair of baggy shorts, a T-shirt that said Florida Smorida, and his hair had just been aloed. He looked wonderful—bright and happy—especially his skin, which hardly managed to contain his body. People can say whatever they like about me, and about Nicky, but he is a handsome boy, maybe a young man, and when I'm a geezer and about to kick it, I doubt I'm going to regret making out with a beautiful guy. I'll probably regret tons of other stuff, but not that, not how he sat on the gunwale, his feet bare, his arm out for me.

"Come here," he said. "What are you doing?"

Drawing, I told him.

"Let me see," he said.

I didn't show him.

"Come here," he said again.

I didn't resist. I didn't pretend I didn't want to kiss him. I hate girls who get coy when the thing they actually want is right in front of them.

I kissed him soft and light, then harder.

—

Forget what I did. Think of a girl or guy you kissed. Think of really kissing them. Think of that thing that happens, where you can hardly contain yourself, you want sex, sort of, but it's also like kissing the entire world, the sand and dirt and leaves and bark and ocean, and you know something about it is biology, just the need to procreate, but something else goes into it, too. I have kissed a few other boys, not many, but a few, and I had never felt the urge I feel with Nicky. It's silly, probably, to try to describe it, but once I stood under a waterfall in upstate New York, and it was bitter cold, and for a second, when I ducked under the water, I wasn't sure I could breathe. Kissing Nicky is better than that. Nicky's kissing is softer than that. My uncle Jeddi used to take a button and put it on string, and then he would twirl it around so the string became coiled. And then, gently, he pulled the string out from both ends and the button began to spin, and the rotation tucked the string tight again, and you pulled again, and it felt like a gyroscope, all syrupy and warm and crazy, and that's the whole thing about kissing Nicky.

"I have to meet Marty," Nicky said after a while.

"Okay," I said, stepping out of his arms. "See you."

"I'd invite you but it's going to be a bunch of guys."

I nodded. I never *ever ever ever* ask him to stay. I *never ever ever ever* become needy.

I grabbed my sketchbook.

"You mad?" he asked.

"You need to be where you need to be."

"It's just one of those things."

"I don't remember asking you for an explanation," I said, keeping it level. "I'll see you around."

He looked at me. Maybe you could say he studied me. And I wish I could say I was being feminine and coy, but I wasn't. I can't stand that stuff. Besides, if my mom taught me anything, she taught me that women have to do their own thing. She calls it the Cinderella Complex, which is a book from back in the 1970s, but it's true anyway. She claims women sit around waiting for Prince Charming to swing by and they waste a ton of their life marking time. Mom talks a ton of gaff, but she's right about that. She is always poking me in the ribs when one of her women friends can't get a guy to do what she wants. She says women should get on with it and stop shuffling their feet, waiting. Nicky isn't Prince Charming, and I don't wear glass slippers, and that's about all I wanted him to understand.

"Later, then," he said.

Then he took off. Just like that.

And if you're wondering if Nicky and I have sex, we don't. I'm not against sex. If I wanted to have sex I would have it with Nicky. Someone once told me that young people having sex is like trying to fill a swimming pool with the drain turned wide open, and I suspect they are right. It simply isn't effective. What Nicky and I have would overwhelm us for about two or three weeks, then it would drain away. If Nicky is frustrated, tough. Meanwhile, I am becoming a first-class kisser. And somewhere down the road, sex is waiting for us. Sometimes if feels like a huge magnet pulling us closer.

2

People asked afterward why I went sailing at night.

I didn't.

I went sailing in the late afternoon, maybe two hours before sunset, when the wind rose perfectly, and the moon hung like the end of a Popsicle that someone pointed at you. Gulls became restless on the water, and the small dace and minnows that moved around the dock posts started flicking around. I watched them for a while and stared deep into the water, dreamy, the way you can sometimes when the sun hits you and your skin is warm and you feel slack and lazy and full. I'm not sure how long I sat there feeling the water lift the boat and set it back down, lift, then settle. I didn't jump up afterward and do a sailor's hornpipe and start throwing off my bowlines. I began preparing the boat almost unconsciously, automatically, and then I pushed off. I didn't hesitate and I didn't start singing a whaling song. I just went sailing.

I headed northwest. I angled for the horizon, out to Kehler's Point, out to where the bay begins to wash and churn. I sat in the stern, the rudder handle in my lap, the spinnaker puffing and pulling like a boy whacking a sheet with a Whiffle bat. The *Mugwump* wallowed. No one would call her a spry boat even on her best days, but on that evening she felt chunky and bored, and I gave her more sail to get her going. The jib began to yank.

A quarter mile out we caught our first true wind. It came across my port bow, which made it simple to exploit. The sails filled, and I felt my heart crack open. It sounds crazy, I know, but whenever the wind finally filled the sails and we began to move, I always felt my heart lift, and I nearly always got teary-eyed and I thought of ridiculous, abstract words, like *magnificence* and *honor* and *truth* and *joy*.

Yo ho ho and a bottle of rum, I whispered.

It's what I always whispered when the boat finally found its way. It settled my heart.

The *Mugwump* began peeling through the water. I turned on my seat and saw the Donaldsons' dock slowly merge with the water behind me, then disappear. I let out my sails and tacked slightly to the north, letting the wind take us at an angle, and we slowly lifted onto the starboard keel. I turned again to watch the moon, and it had lifted a few fingers higher above the horizon. If it had been darker, the moon would have put a path on the water. A moon trail.

The *Mugwump* picked up speed and finally we began hissing through the water, the chop chucking us under the starboard side of the bow, the wind pushing at my hair. A tin cup rolled somewhere on the deck, and I puzzled for a second about what it could be. It didn't sound important, so I ignored it and looked over the bay. Harry Boyd's fishing boat, the *Yoda,* chugged along to the south, heading to port, and an enormous yacht, a forty-footer at least, forged ahead of me to the north. The yacht had its running lights going—red, port; green, starboard—and I used its bow as a navigation point for a minute or two. I even recited the little poem I learned when I first began sailing:

When green and red I see ahead,
I turn to starboard and show my red:
Green to green, red to red,
Perfect safety—go ahead.

But if to starboard red appear,
It is my duty to keep clear—
To act as judgment says is proper:
To port or starboard, back or stop her.

It took me twenty minutes to get close enough to Kehler's Point to see the cormorants perched in the mangrove trees. They resembled old men wearing overcoats too large for them. I stood in the stern when I saw them and hooted, and they looked up, but that was all. The sun had begun to set behind them. Gulls flashed around them like bits of light.

I lashed the rudder and sat quietly for a few minutes, letting the boat follow the wind, the thrum of the water steady underneath. I thought of Nicky and of Mom, and I thought of raspberry sherbet, a big bowl of it, red and cool and clean, and I thought of an English project I had due, one on the writer Marjorie Kinnan Rawlings and how she had moved down to Florida's central region and had dedicated herself to writing, leaving her husband behind—no Cinderella waiting around for Prince Charming—and how she described going out to build smoke pots to warm the orange trees in a neighbor's grove. *Cross Creek*, her memoir was called. And I had read *The Yearling*, too, which was too sad for words, but beautiful, too, and how I knew I would get an A on the project because I am good at those things and serious about them, and how my teacher, Mrs. Pointer, had a little secret language she used when she handed papers back to me, telling me I could do good things in my life, that it was okay to love books and drawing and paper. Then I thought some more about sherbet, how the taste of it always felt like pirates, and I thought of how my sails must look to Harry in the *Yoda* or even to the people on the enormous yacht, and how the sea is curved and arched, so you are never sailing on a flat plane but on the back of a sleeping animal, the ocean is just an animal, and the wind is its snoring.

Crazy thoughts. Sailing thoughts.

If you hold your hand out at arm's length, with your fingers together, and place it between the horizon and the sun, then each finger represents fifteen minutes.

Try it the next time you are outside near sunset. It works, I promise.

I had three fingers of sunlight left, forty-five minutes, when I started to come about. If you don't know anything about sailing, coming about can be tricky. You have to change the angle of the sail to the wind, so if the wind blew behind you to begin with, you must swing the sail to starboard to bring the bow around to port. The boom, which anchors the bottom of the sail, swings hard. It takes a little while to get the feeling of coming about, but once you get the knack it becomes instinctive and automatic, like driving a car or riding a bike. You don't have to pay strict attention because your muscle-memory skills kick into gear.

And that, probably, caused my downfall.

Because when you turn the bow, you also risk taking waves directly on your side. When you take waves on your side, you risk getting swamped, or rolled. Of course, boats have heavy keels to prevent rolling or tumbling. But anything a human can make, the sea can undo, and if you sail long enough, the sea will win, always, every time. The sea won't take any pleasure in it anymore than a wind finds joy in snapping a tree branch.

I wasn't paying attention. The jib luffed. Then for an instant, a long, horrible instant, I knew something had gone terribly wrong. A wave, maybe a rogue wave, suddenly lifted and rose to my starboard, and I turned to it as if someone had just insulted me in a way I hadn't expected.

I remember reaching my hand out to brace myself, my left hand against the port gunwale, and I said something like *whoa* or *yikes*, but that sounded silly. Then in a massive shrug, the *Mugwump* turned almost perpendicular to the surface of the ocean, like a trick boat standing on its nose. The keel yawed out from under the boat, and I felt the boat ring like the knell of a heavy pendulum, *bong, bong, bong*, and the boat kept turning and turning. I thought, *This isn't right, this can't be, the keel will catch me, the keel will pull me back*, but then the port gunwale went underwater, and I thought, *Did I hit a whale? Have I rammed something?* Because the *Mugwump* had never handled this way, not even close. I looked up to see the topmost tip of the mast moving past parallel to the sea, the small blue banner I used to detect wind direction dipped into a second large wave, and I knew I was going over.

I grabbed the rudder handle, and that probably worked against me because the force of my body slowly levering it forced the rudder blade to twist. At the same instant, I felt my body lifting on the rudder, gradually sliding toward the water like someone holding up a tablecloth to contain a spill. I threw my weight back and tried to grab something, anything, to keep me onboard, and I thought, *No no no no no*. I wasn't scared, not at that moment. I was simply furious at myself that I hadn't paid close attention, and that the *Mugwump* had betrayed me, and that I was going in the water with forty-five minutes until darkness.

Stupid, stupid, stupid, I thought.

The boat paused, then it turtled. The sail tucked under the boat, caught the force of a wave or a current and it lifted the keel out of the water. I knew the *Mugwump* was not self-righting, meaning it might or might not pop back up to its correct position. Before I could even think that thought through, I knew I had to dive away from the boat. It sounds crazy, but I knew the boat could keep turning and the keel could snap down on me like a flyswatter, or the sail could catch me, or any of about a million things could hit me. Even then, I didn't do it. I thought, *This can't be happening*, but then the boat tilted one more time and I felt a deep, dark resolve shape itself in my belly. The boat turned lazily, as if it couldn't quite make up its mind, and I heard a crash in the cabin, then a second crash, then a hissing sound of something rending.

Then I jumped.

The water slapped my Chuck Taylors, the sneakers I always wore when I sailed. I heard something pop behind me, followed by a large sucking sound, and suddenly the mast snapped in two. The broken end of the mast jabbed straight up, and if I had stayed aboard, if I hadn't jumped, I would have taken it square in the chest. The sail snapped off and slid into the water like a sheet of paper following a breeze.

The bow dipped straight down and the boat bucked. Something made a horrible, grinding sound, and when it finished, the boat had its bow down, looking like a duck sticking its butt in the air while its head feeds on grass at the bottom of a lake. It happened in almost one complete dip. Then for a minute the water swirled it around and the boat looked playful, kind of merry, and I treaded water and watched. One thing I counted on: a Boston Whaler will not sink. That was the feature of the boat that made my mother comfortable with my solo sailing. If it couldn't sink, you had a good chance of being okay, and the structure of the boat came loaded with wedges of foam. I had reminded her of that feature a dozen times. And now the boat appeared as if someone wanted to yank it beneath the waves, a bobber following a trout.

I didn't feel anything. I didn't feel conscious of anything. I wanted to understand what had happened, what was going on, and my adrenaline had kicked my system so high I existed in an openmouthed, panting sort of way. It looked, for a second, as if the boat might rise out of the water and snap back at me, just as the mast had done, but then it simply slid farther down, and I realized suddenly that it wasn't going anywhere.

It's stuck, I said.

It's stuck, I thought, like an echo.

Which didn't make any sense.

Sailing is about motion. The water moves. The wind moves. The tides move. The birds move. The boat moves. The sail moves. The moon moves. The sun moves.

Things do not stick.

I smiled. It sounds odd, probably, but I did. One time

when I reached for a plastic ketchup bottle, I hit it with the side of my hand. The ketchup bottle turned a cartwheel and ended right back on its proper end. You could try to do that a million times and you wouldn't get it to do the same trick again. And you couldn't get a sailboat to stick in one place in the middle of the bay if you sailed a thousand years.

Two fingers of sun remained.

I had to slow things down. I had been treading water like crazy and only now, minutes later, did I remember I wore a life jacket. I took a deep breath and for a second I put my head back and rested. Personal flotation devices are designed to keep your head above water, so I closed my eyes for a second and tried not to think of anything. *I'm alive,* I kept repeating. *I'm okay.*

Then I used my mantra. It's a meditation word, and you can think what you like about meditation, call it stupid or hippie-dippy, but I was happy to have that calming word, which I won't repeat here because it belongs to me and only me, but which I whispered and repeated until the whole world became just that word. I let it fill my head, as it can, and I forced myself to relax my body, to lean back, and rest.

When I opened my eyes, I had drifted thirty feet away from the *Mugwump.*

A little rumble of panic kicked in and I swam two strokes fast toward the boat before I regained my composure. *Easy,*

I told myself. But I didn't want to lose the boat. I swam with my head out of the water and got back within ten feet of it and paused. I couldn't be under the boat if it rolled. Then I thought about how Mr. Baines, a retired greenhouse manager who sailed and had taught me some things about boats, used to say sailing is about responsibility. He said in almost any activity you do in life you can either blame someone else or ask for help, but in sailing the buck always stopped with you. The weather could work against you, true, but the boat had to be your responsibility, and that attitude helped me in a general way, made me not pass things on or wait for help.

Mr. Baines would say: something must be holding your boat and you don't know what it is.

I knew what I had to do.

I took a big breath and stuck my head under the water. Immediately salt stung my eyes and I couldn't see more than a few feet. I needed more light, I realized, and I needed to get closer.

Think, think, think, I thought.

I needed the boat released. And I needed it quickly. I treaded water on the lee side, meaning the boat broke the current for me, but I didn't want to be on that side if the boat popped up suddenly. The current and waves would flick the boat right on top of me, so I forced myself to swim slowly around to the other side, stopping now and then to stick my face underwater. Each time I put my face under, I had to refocus, letting the water and movement slow down until I could catch glimpses of the *Mugwump*. By the tenth time I put my head under, I had pieced together a rough idea of what might have happened.

The *Mugwump* had impaled itself on something huge and rusty at the bottom of the bay. The object had gone aground, even though it was near no ground. I determined that much. I could see it directly below the boat, a faded orange, though its outline remained indistinct. It glimmered like coral or the back of a rock, but I sensed it had been dumped there, that it was man-made. Maybe someone had lost a motor, or someone had jettisoned an enormous hunk of scrap metal in the middle of the night and the metal had lodged in the shallow bay, lifting one dangerous end to passing boats. The metal may have rested beneath the waves for years, never proving a problem, until a specific set of circumstances ganged up to jam the *Mugwump*'s bow down hard in one unfortunate instant. Maybe a bigger than average wave had hit me, or maybe the rusted hunk had caused a backwash of some sort, permitting the bow to dive deeper than it ordinarily would. One thing I told myself: however it happened no longer mattered because that is in the past, and I am here.

———

Here's what I knew about shipwrecks five minutes before I experienced one:

1. Stay with the boat.

2. Do not drink salt water. You may drink your own urine in small quantities.
3. The sea eventually brings everything to land, dead or alive.
4. Do not panic. Think. Use your head.
5. Exposure to the sun, the wind, and salt will dehydrate you. Dehydration kills people more quickly than anything else in a shipwreck.

Here's what I knew about my personal shipwreck:
1. I had left a note for Mrs. Donaldson so someone would know I hadn't returned.
2. I was in the bay, not the open ocean, and plenty of boats passed my way all the time.
3. I couldn't be more than a mile or two from land in any direction.
4. I was likely to drift south and west if I didn't stay with the boat, which meant I would move away from land and toward bigger water.
5. The weather forecast called for a calm night.
6. I had been right about one thing: if I didn't make it through the night, I was glad I kissed Nicky as much as I had.
7. When a big thing is happening to you, you can't quite believe it. It doesn't seem big to you. It's just a thing you are going through. Big things happen to other people. What happens to you is nuts and bolts, just daily stuff.

3

The sun went down.

The wind stopped for a second and the water seemed to calm. I looked at the western horizon and watched the top edge of the sun slip under the sea. Everything turned quiet and still, and I listened as the water slapped the sides of the *Mugwump*, and I thought about praying, then thought I shouldn't, that was a chicken thing to do, because I didn't believe in God when I was safe and dry on land, and if I did believe in God then I had to believe God wanted me to be in the water, He had wanted to wreck my ship, He had placed the hunk of metal before me, and He had also wished for wars to occur, and cancer and leukemia, and I couldn't square that in my head, so I thought of sherbet instead, a bright red scoop of it in a white ceramic bowl, and I dreamed of lifting that spoon to my mouth, the first silvery taste of the sherbet washing away everything else, and I thought of Nicky, and how he was a nice person, a decent guy even though other people thought he just wanted to sex me up, he was okay, just a gentle guy who liked the sun and messing around on boats, and he didn't mean any harm to anyone, and his life hadn't been easy, not at all, and I wondered what Mrs. Pointer would think when she heard I survived a shipwreck, and I wondered what the center of Florida was like, the heart of it where Marjorie Rawlings had lived, and I tried to picture Flag, the yearling fawn, and what it must have been like a hundred years ago in Florida, before cars buzzed everywhere, and before a million boats flocked around the shores, and I wondered what Marjorie Rawlings would have to say about my story, what she thought about when she looked out her window at the Florida wilds and she sent her manuscripts off to New York, to an editor who told her the work was fantastic, beautiful, and it was, she had made up a story that would outlive her, and I wondered if I hadn't started on my own story, that the sea had given me a story, and I turned in the water away from the setting sun and forced myself to face the moon, the bright orange moon that now rose over the mainland.

And that was when something bumped me.

Something hit my leg.

I felt a scream climbing up my ribcage, bone by bone, and I couldn't help paddling faster, just treading water as if I could chase whatever it was away. It felt like having a spider on me, only bigger and more gluey, and I whispered, *No, no, no, no.*

Because something had bumped me.

I did not have to think twice about what might have bumped me. I had seen enough nature programs, and I had listened to a hundred stories from Nicky and his buddies when they got together and talked about fishing and the sea and surfing and diving and big fish following boats. Everyone knows who bumps who.

Sharks bump people.

Sharks bump objects, like people reaching into a cookie jar in a dark kitchen. They want to know what is inside.

"Sharks don't want to hurt you," Nicky used to say, quoting the guy who wrote *Jaws*. "They just want to eat you."

Nothing personal. Everything is biology in the end.

I tried to remember what attracts sharks, what draws them in, but it seemed like blood is the main thing, and some sort of electromagnetic current, and I remembered you should not flap and flail and behave as though you were injured. It took everything inside me to slow my body down, to relax, because now the ocean had turned dark, and the whole world suddenly divided between up and down. Down is where the sharks lived, and up was where I lived, and I wanted my body out of the shark's world. Above all, I hoped a bull shark had not found me, because bulls did not have souls, according to Nicky. Bulls ate what they found, they swam like greedy arms looking for food to bring back to an insatiable mouth, for the appetite of the whole world, and you could worry about great whites all you liked, and about tigers and hammerheads, but the real stomach of the sea was the bull shark, a frowning, gray animal that tore arms off swimmers and swam away with legs chucking sideways down their endless guts.

I swam to the *Mugwump* and put my thighs against its flank as much as I could and I tried not to breathe. I tried to be part of the ship, not a body, and maybe it was the companionship of the boat or the slower, more rational part of my mind dancing back into the light, but I realized that a bump did not necessarily mean a shark. It could have been nearly anything, a fish, a mullet, a piece of flotsam from the *Mugwump*. It could have been a log from the mainland or a coconut, and maybe it had been nothing at all. It did not stand to reason that a shark would find you in the first quarter hour you were in the water. Statistically it would have been a fluke, a crazy ironic coincidence, like lightning burning a *Z* in Zorro's shoulder blade, or a boat impaling itself on a rusty engine part.

But sharks existed. And if a shark got you, it wouldn't be an easy death. It would bite and it would tear and you wouldn't be able to kid yourself that it wasn't happening, that you weren't being eaten. You would see its gray back, its dorsal fin shaking as its mouth pulled your limbs in like licorice whips. A cougar or tiger would snap your neck, and an elephant would crush you with its feet. Even an alligator would roll you until you drowned and it would be a lousy way to go, but better than being eaten by a shark. You might be able to look a shark in the eye as it chewed its way higher on your body, and then it would pull back, great bloody blooms following it back into the sea. And it would come again, and again, and you would feel each attack, the final death bite far away, and empty like the last fireworks on a summer night.

After staying next to the boat for a minute or two, I realized that I hadn't really tried to climb back inside it. In a TV story, of course, the narrator should know right away how to figure tactics out like that, but I promise it is a different thing when you are suddenly in the water, and the boat you had trusted has gone under, and any wave could flick the boat on top of you, and maybe a shark had taken your measure, and so anyone who likes to think they can do better is free to criticize me. But if you've ever been in a hairy situation, I bet you won't. Things happen fast, and they happen hard, and it's not easy to know what you should have done until you are doing it. Deep down, a quiet part of your mind tries to reassure you that *this is not happening*, and that's the first thing to conquer. Maybe that's shock. Maybe it's a skewed survival method. But until you slow down and start to weigh your options, you're nothing more than a hunk of biological matter ready to return to the natural system.

I turned and hugged the front shoulder of the *Mugwump*. Water kept trying to separate me from the boat, to pull me away, but I held on and looked up, attempting to see what I could do. The sailboat had settled a little, so that maybe now it reached out of the water at a 30-degree slope, but the stern of the boat, where you could easily climb in, was sticking up six feet above the surface. That left the front of the boat available to me, but the sides of the *Mugwump* didn't provide any handholds except a cleat at the top edge of my reach. Because I was in water, I couldn't raise my body. I couldn't get any jump, like the bounce you might take just before you swing up onto a tree branch. A friend of Nicky's named Frank once told us that rock climbing is in your legs, not your arms, that most people's arms can't do too much, because your legs possess the muscles that lift you day in and day out, and I knew he had been right. I couldn't climb because I had no way to get my legs onto the boat, and even grabbing at some of the rope that dangled into the water didn't help. It's a fantasy to think you can pull yourself up on a thin line, hand over hand, but I did hold to the rope for a second and looped it through my life jacket. The rope would keep me with the boat, I figured, and rescue searchers could find a boat easier than they could find a lone swimmer drifting in a life jacket. The sail had gone under, so searchers would find it more difficult to spot the *Mugwump*, but at least they would have a chance to see me. An orange life-jacket dot in a thousand miles of blue is microscopic from the air.

And eventually, I thought, the boat would have to fall back into the water. It had to. Nothing stayed still forever in the ocean. Even enormous ships that sunk eventually broke to pieces. The sea could not be stalled forever. The sea claimed docks and beaches, and sometimes, when it whipped up, it slammed an entire city, like New Orleans.

Or it crashed onto the beach in a killer tsunami, washing away entire villages, chasing people into the mountains to try to escape. A boat dangling on a rusty spar didn't stand a chance of staying there long.

Just long enough, a dark voice inside me answered.

Long enough to drown.

Long enough for a bull shark to tear off my leg.

For a while, I did nothing. I'm not sure how long it lasted. But I hugged the boat and stared ahead, and part of me wonders if I wasn't making up my mind to live. That's all. I know some time went by, but how much is hard to say. I stared for a while at the white straps on my life jacket. They floated in the water, and I thought, how pretty they were, how gracefully they moved. My head emptied. Religions talk about confirmations or initiation rites, and maybe it's too much to hang on such a small moment, but something changed inside me. I was one kind of Lolly before, one after. It happened without conscious thought. When I woke, when I came to, nothing had changed but everything had changed. I had seen myself disappear from the earth, ceased to exist, then I had returned, reborn, and it had all happened in ten breaths.

Then I had another idea. It took time to seep into my head. I had to figure things out without any perspective or distance. When I finally did, a great giddy feeling took life in my belly.

Of course, I told myself.

I needed to go to the front of the *Mugwump* and climb up it.

Simple mechanics. If the front of the boat had rammed into the rusted crud beneath the surface, then I could go to the front of the boat and climb up, using whatever held it as a foot brace. That made sense. I could probably walk up it, or at least crawl, and I kicked myself that I hadn't thought of it sooner. The best place to get into the boat had to be its lowest point, and right now that was the bow on the starboard side. It hit me like a big *duh*.

I unlashed myself from the rope and used my hands to guide myself around to the front of the boat. I kept my legs fitted as close to the boat as possible. I could not let myself picture the shark circling, its body aware of me through a strip of sensation on its sides and face, its head turning slowly back and forth like the mouth of a vacuum cleaner. Hand over hand I went around to the bow, easing around the final corner until I came directly in front of the boat.

How easy!

I nearly laughed. All this time I had assumed I had to climb in over the side, yet now it became obvious that, even though I might get splashed around, the boat formed a ramp out of the water. Just like that. I waited for a wave to shape behind me, then I let its height push me toward the deck of the boat. I went up and hit my head on the cuddy top, the cabin, and I shoved my body forward. I reached for a handhold, anything, my body lunging, and

I grabbed a rope, something, and a great whoop shoved through my system. I felt solid boat underneath me at last, and I kept scrambling up, jerking my body as hard as I could up, up, up. I whacked my knee on something, then felt the rope snatch at my wrist, and the waves behind me pushed and pulled me. Twice I had to stop climbing in order to let the waves pull back, then I leaned farther up the slope of boat, and I felt an uncontrollable shiver pass over me as my feet remained in the water. Bulls, I knew, sometimes climbed onto surfboards, reached up with their saw-toothed mouths, and grabbed surfers, and I let a warble come out of me, a crazy, head-snapping, buzzing chill, and I desperately pulled my feet up.

My weight pushed the boat off the metal spar. The boat had been hanging by a thread, and my weight, as simple as that, pushed it free.

I heard it scrape like the world's biggest table being dragged across a stone floor, and then the boat jammed backward, off the spar, and I grabbed hard with both hands. I was in a downward dog Yoga pose, hands and toes, and I rooted myself there and waited while the boat shifted under me and began to come back to center. The keel slammed or broke off, I wasn't sure, but then the boat lifted and shot toward its stern, and the great sickle of the boom lifted out of the water on the port side and swung around with such force that I did not see it coming. Maybe I had thought the boom was gone with the rest of the mast; and maybe I had given in to the joy of being onboard again, but the boom snapped toward me like the arm of a huge man turning in his sleep, uncoiling and snapping with force. The momentum of the waves, the force of the boat's shoving backward, the freedom the boom suddenly gained as the boat righted combined to send the boom singing toward me. Positioned as I was, on hands and knees above the cuddy, the boom hit me in the forehead with the force and measure of a baseball bat.

4

I woke to find the boat gone.

Or the boat stayed and I had gone.

Either way, I was alone in the sea in the dark and the *Mugwump* had disappeared.

I was a dot in the ocean. And the ocean was a dot on the earth. And the earth was a dot in the solar system. And the solar system was a dot in the universe. And the universe might be a dot inside a larger world, for all we know, and if we finally accepted our dot-ness, our insignificance, then we gained peace, or at least comfort. And raspberry sherbet is no more or less important than anything else, when you consider our dot-ness, and so to take a spoonful of sherbet and let it freeze then warm the roof of your mouth is as significant as any other action, marriage, or birth, or Christmas, and so each thing is important and meaningless at the same time, and if you can get around that, truly accept it, then life becomes smooth and beautiful. That's what I knew. That's what I understood.

—

I did not scream or cry. I waited to feel my heart beating. I waited to feel my lungs going in and out, and I waited to see the moon. I felt my hair drifting on the surface of the ocean. I did not give up.

I gave in.

There is a difference. I woke slowly, my hand moving up to my forehead where an enormous lump had formed. I felt nauseated, too, and maybe I had thrown up. I closed my eyes and I felt as though I could turn slowly inside out, turn until I was nothing except a hollow tube in the ocean, a blank, effortless piece of kelp drifting in the sea. It made no sense to struggle. I did not feel panic or danger or loss. Maybe I had accepted my own death at last and that did not feel to be the worst thing. Death is not the worst thing, I know now, and I am no longer afraid of it. But on that night in the ocean I felt death comfortably beside me, and I understood that I was a thing, an animal, a product of carbon, and that someday I would exist no longer. And of course I wanted sherbet and to see Nicky and my mother, but another part of me, the animal part, accepted what had happened. I did not accuse myself of being stupid, or poorly prepared, or a lousy sea captain. Fate had taken an interest in my life somehow, and I accepted that, just as I accepted that my legs now dangled in the dark, dark sea, and sharks could have me. I knew I must be bleeding and the vomit in my mouth must have purged into the sea, and so the other animals could have me. A squirrel's death in the road is sad only for a moment, and I comprehended that now, likely, my turn had come. I did not feel a grand connection to the universe except to look at the moon and let it hypnotize me slightly, the waves lifting me and rocking me in the yoke of my life jacket.

The spirit of Lolly Emmerson existed, was present, was here, and was at peace.

Motion. Everything was in motion. That's another thing I understood. I drifted on the sea, and the currents moved me, and the wind blew gently across the wave tops, and the sky moved, the stars circled in relation to the earth, and the moon came and went, drifted across the sky as if pulled by chariots, and clouds, even at night, did their business and passed. Birds flew in the wind, and deep down, where the wind passed over the birds' wings, an entire physics problem existed—lift and drag and pull. All movement. The top part of my body moved, and my legs drifted slightly behind me, so that, even around my frame, the elements moved differently, at different paces, and nothing remained still and constant. My hair moved, and my hands, and the white straps of the life jacket, and the soggy laces of my Chuck Taylors. On land, we once believed we remained stationary, but that was an illusion. The earth spun, and the wind redistributed soil, and ice in the northern climates reached down into cracks and pried up the dirt and rock, and volcanoes spewed new islands into the sea, where they steamed and hissed and finally solidified, only to have the sea begin pulling them apart again.

—

And as I dreamed about motion, I heard the first blow.

Later, naturally, people did not listen to the first part. They wanted the Lassie part, the girl and her dog part. But what you must hear if you are to understand is that I had let go before he arrived.

Imagine the darkness, the waves, and the sound of breathing.

I turned slowly. I could no longer feel my legs. My body shook with the cold of being immersed for so long. I stopped moving and listened. A moment later I heard a breath, a short explosive blow.

Dolphin, I thought.

Come to me, I whispered. *Please help me.*

And he did. But it was not a dolphin.

His huge body suddenly appeared beside me. I felt no fear. A thousand years and a thousand seas had brought him to me. I reached my hand to him and slowly, painfully, crawled on top of his wide back.

It was a manatee. And he had come for me.

He knew.

He knew I had given in and he understood I would not survive without him. He had found me, perhaps not deliberately, but with the detachment of a man on a journey who takes time to perform a small chore. As soon as my hand touched his skin, and I felt the steadiness of his enormous body beneath me, my heart lifted. I did not feel a moment's fear or hesitation. I spread my arms and wrapped them as far around him as I could. Whether we moved or not, I could hardly tell. I felt delirious and exhausted, and I realized, belatedly, that I had probably drifted close to a shoreline. Manatees, I knew, lived near the shore, and I clung to him, listening for breaking surf. The moon threw a path before him, and you can say I am crazy, but I began chanting a song. It had no words, but it sounded the way I had heard Indians chant, a calling out to spirits older than any we can name, and the sea, I promise, spilled in and out of my mouth. I moved my hands over his body and he slowly dipped down, undulating, and my right hand searched for him and I found a gash in his back. A propeller cut. I knew about these, about how outboards tore through the water and chopped enormous hunks of flesh from their bodies, and now my hand searched inside the gash for a handhold.

And that was how we traveled. My hand in his old wound.

I have tried to picture what we must have looked like.

Dark, dark, dark, and the huge bulk of him underneath me. You would not have seen him. In the moonlight, in the white phosphorescence, you would have seen a girl riding through the chop, her head barely above the water, her face sometimes straining to get air. My movement would not have made sense to an onlooker. A human could not pass so quickly through the water. I tried to keep my hand resting lightly on his wound. It had healed, but the gash remained, a furrow where the water, when he rose, occasionally pooled and lingered before it swirled back into the sea. At those moments when his shoulder cleared the water, I spread my arms and held him, petting him quietly, and his skin felt like a great inner tube, only warmer. I tried to keep my body squarely above his and I allowed the water to support me as much as possible. At times he slowed, and then I felt an enormous surge of water catch us and move us slowly forward; at other times he seemed to be determined, and his flippers moved water toward me like bats of pressure, like air turned to liquid and blown toward me.

The song that I had sung sank inside my body and stayed there.

Once or twice, in the churn of the water around me, I heard surf. I could not be certain, though, and each time, when I listened, I felt the surge of the manatee under me, and I committed myself again to being present in the moment. It's important to understand this: I did not navigate, I did not search for landmarks, I did not try to predict an outcome. In their questions and comments afterward, people wanted to attribute my survival to my sharp observations or my sailing skills, but they missed the most basic point: I survived because I let go.

A minute, two minutes, and then he lifted his head and blew air from his nostrils in a loud, quick burst. Sometimes he stayed on the surface, and sometimes he drifted down, his buoyancy never letting him go too deep. Slowly, I began to realize we were not alone. A second manatee swam on our right, and a third, somewhere behind, occasionally shot a spray of air in our direction. I did not turn my head to see. I knew they were there. And they knew I had joined them.

5

Here is what happened on land.

Mrs. Donaldson returned from the restaurant with her husband, Joe, and she called my mother and told her the boat was still out. My mother said to call back in a half hour if it hadn't returned. Mrs. Donaldson did. Mrs. Donaldson had also found my note saying I was going to make a loop toward Kehler's Point. Mr. Donaldson, Joe, went down to wait on the dock to have a cigar and stand lookout. He had a large flash beam that carried his eyesight out pretty far into the bay. He smoked about half of the cigar and kept scanning the water, but he didn't see any sign of me.

My mother called Mr. Twitchell, a party-boat operator and a friend of the family's whose dock was only a quarter mile down from the Donaldsons', who told her not to worry. He said on a full moon night I was probably simply enjoying a sail. Who wouldn't? He promised, though, not to go to bed until he heard I was back safe at the Donaldsons'. My mother wasn't satisfied. She asked if he would go to his boat, the *Molly May*, and monitor his radio so that he could find out if anyone had seen me. Mr.

Twitchell said he would, but he didn't go to the dock until later. He figured that it was just my mom being overly protective. He was from Louisiana originally, and he liked to listen to LSU sports via the Internet, and he had been listening to a talk show with the LSU football coach when my mom called. He wasn't going to leave the show to go running off looking for a girl who would likely return before he could get his boat launched. By then, if I have the timing correct, I was in the water after being swept off the boat by the boom.

Mrs. Donaldson walked down to the dock to confer with her husband. They talked for a while, trying to sort it out. They did a few calculations about time and distance, but they couldn't come up with anything conclusive. Finally Mrs. Donaldson called my mom one last time and urged her to report a missing boat to the Coast Guard.

My mother began to cry and Mrs. Donaldson said it was just a precaution, no reason to get alarmed, but that they should put some plans in motion. My mother agreed and got in her car armed with her cell phone and drove to the Donaldsons'. By that time my mom raised the Coast Guard operator, who said he would report the boat late to port, but that they would wait three hours or more before sending out anyone to look. My mother threw a tizz.

What do you mean wait three hours, why do we pay taxes, what's the point of the Coast Guard if you're not going to look, yes, yes, of course, no, she is a good sailor, no, she doesn't run late, who is this, what is your name, who is your supervisor?

And so on.

She called Mr. Twitchell, forgetting that she had asked him to be at his boat and not at all surprised when he picked up in the house. He said he would make some calls. His guilt over not checking in the first place made him fairly efficient from that point forward. He put out a radio call to anyone who had spotted the *Mugwump*, a Boston Whaler Harpoon, white sail with green trim, sailing from the mainland at approximately four thirty. It took a roundabout way, but eventually the call came to Harry Boyd, captain of the *Yoda*, who had already taken two six-teen-ounce Budweisers on board as ballast, and he said, yes, yes, he had seen the sailboat, the hippie girl who hung around Nicky, sailing right along just fine toward Kehler's Point. What was her name? the captain wondered aloud. When Mr. Twitchell said *Lolly*, Harry Boyd said, that's right, as if he had come up with the name after all.

Patrolman Lewis, a jerk who most of the kids in the area hated, swung by to check on things. Apparently he had listened in on the radio when Mr. Twitchell sent out a call. Patrolman Lewis was a short doofus, a twenty-year-old kid who had never been cool in high school or anywhere else but whose uncle was a big wheel with the state police, so he pulled strings and got Patrolman Lewis hired. Patrolman Lewis looked like a wet golden retriever, all pressed down and skin showing where you wouldn't expect it. His brows connected and he had eczema or psoriasis on his elbows, so whenever you saw him you thought he might be flaking away like an old painted wall. The fact that he was a cop was the only reason anyone paid any attention to him at all. Without a badge he would have been a complete zero. With a badge he was zero squared, and he kind of knew it, and that made him more horrible, and his middle name was Louis and so, naturally, everyone called him Louis Lewis.

Anyway, he came by and squawked his car a couple of times, walked around to the back of the Donaldsons' and investigated the mooring. He said he had heard about the boat being delayed, and he wondered if anyone knew my status, and then he didn't do much except get in the way. He wondered aloud if anyone had seen Nicky, because in his experience young couples sometimes forget about time, at which point my mother told him he was an obnoxious little twit and to get the freak out of her sight, and not to come back unless he had something to contribute. According to Mrs. Donaldson, he tried to do a slow meltaway, as if it had been his idea to take off and that my mom was just an emotional car wreck, and she said under different circumstances she would have laughed out loud at the way he skulked away.

That's the way things stood for about a half hour. Mrs. Donaldson brewed a big pot of coffee and they sat out in the backyard with the bug zapper frying bugs now and then, and they watched the bay and waited for some sign of me. It started to get weird, according to Mrs. Donaldson. She said in the beginning you more or less figure there has been some mistake, some miscommunication, but afterward, as it started to sink in that I wasn't coming right back, the mood changed. It started to stretch, is the way she put it, and everyone became conscious that this was real. This was happening. A person they knew—not some TV story or a headline from the paper—might have gone missing. Nothing you can do prepares you for that, for the powerless feeling you get, and Mrs. Donaldson said she thought about throwing bread on the water, the way Catholics are taught to do, that if you cast your bread upon the water it returns to you. Crazy notions like that, she said. And everyone just sat in the backyard as if it were any other day and they had just finished cocktails. She said she almost wished Patrolman Louis Lewis would return so they could all gang up on him and let out some pressure.

After about forty-five minutes, Mr. Twitchell called to say he had decided to launch and take a run out to Kehler's Point. He said it wouldn't hurt to take a look, and what likely happened was a problem with a sail or something small but disabling to the boat. Mr. Donaldson, who knew little about boats despite living next to the sea, went with him as crew. When Mr. Twitchell's boat stopped by the Donaldsons' dock, Mr. Donaldson jumped on and took his large searchlight with him. They promised to be in close radio contact and that they wouldn't be long. The whole trip would only take an hour, maybe less, Mr. Twitchell said. Then, while Mr. Donaldson climbed aboard, Mr. Twitchell told my mother it wouldn't hurt to give the Coast

Guard another ring. Just to get their thoughts or to hear if they had had any reports. Hearing that was a knife in my mother's heart.

Nicky heard from Mrs. Twitchell that the boat had gone missing. She had given her husband a jacket and a thermos of coffee, then drove over to sit with my mom and Mrs. Donaldson. On her way to her car, she happened on Nicky, who had been pedaling toward my dock after his visit with his buddies.

She's not there, she called to Nicky. *Her boat's gone missing.*

People like to be the first to tell news, even if they are nice people, and even if the news is bad.

What? he asked, but then he didn't ask for clarification.

Sometimes we ask *what* when we've heard perfectly well what someone said but are not prepared to absorb it.

6

My hand began to slip.

The cold had finally taken a grip on me and I could not get my shivering under control. Deep in my body, down by my spine, a feeling like a wire being stretched started to grind and move through the muscles along my backbone. After the wire had stretched, it suddenly twanged, and I felt a shudder shoot through my body until the ends of the wire caught in my muscles again and began to tighten. I knew I had symptoms of hypothermia.

Slower, I whispered, but the manatee did not go slower.

Twice I lifted my head and tried to see a landmark. I suspected it was pointless and it proved to be, but I couldn't resist. I tried to crane my head and see, my eyes squinting against the salt and the sting of water. The second time, I stared straight up at the stars, trying to find Polaris, but then my hand slipped off the manatee altogether and for an instant I rested suspended in the water, the smooth tube of his body passing away from me.

Let go, I thought.

I did not feel peaceful this time. I felt myself giving up, which is different from giving in, and before I could let the ocean take me I grabbed and caught the manatee where his hips would have been if he had been a human. He did not seem to register my change in position. I could continue with him, or leave, and he would not stop or move faster. Maybe to him I was simply kelp, or a wand of sea grass lolling across his lower body.

Slowly, with care, I worked my way up his body. I waited until he surfaced for breath, then climbed higher, reaching forward until I had my hand once more in his wound. I berated myself for letting go in the first place, but a siren voice whispered sweetly in my ear that I should let go, remove my hand, and abandon myself to the open sea.

I shivered. My jaws ached from shivering.

The darker side of my soul reasoned that I could not go on much longer. The voice told me I was cold, and that the manatee might travel for miles without coming near the shore, and that I had not been bumped by a bull shark, that was silly, it had been a coconut, that was all, and if I let go I could rest at last and the cold would lull me and my legs would dangle down into the dark, dark sea, but I did not need my legs, I didn't need anything any longer if I simply dropped my hand from the manatee's back. The cold would leave me. My cares would leave me, and though I could picture my mother, a sweet, tired face, she would be all right without me. Better than all right, really. Her life would be simpler without me, and my body would blend with the blue molecules of the ocean, and tomorrow, when the sun came forward, I would drift like a white bobbin, the small fishes first taking my brows and tongue, and then my ears would turn to pudding and I would hear the sea, the sea would be inside my head, and I would drift farther to sea until a shark approached and knuckled my ribs with its teeth, tearing off a chunk that did not hurt any longer, felt nothing any longer, but my flesh became shark and fin and cartilage and swam away into the deeper ocean like a cat's tail slicing from side to side on a slick linoleum floor.

I am cold, I told the manatee.

The manatee did not answer. Instead I heard rain. Or what I believed to be rain. Then slowly I realized we had come through a school of flying fish. I saw them zing into the air and fly for a moment, and I knew that something chased them, something deadly, because they took to the air to escape. They came like a web of grass before a mower, scattering and pelting, and one grazed my shoulder, another hit my leg, and I kicked to stay with the manatee because something down deep hungered. Something chased, and something ran, and I hoped it was a smaller predator, a barracuda or a redfish, because I could not let it be a shark. I did not want to conjure the gun-metal sides of a shark, the silent tail thrash, and so I pushed my body closer to the manatee and the flying fish started to slow, their reentry into the water like knives slicing in and resuming a cut, and I closed my eyes and tried to become part of the manatee. Probably insane, I know, but I sent my soul, my being, down my arm and into the manatee, and I felt a little crazy doing it, but it worked, too, and I became manatee for a moment. Just a moment. But by then the flying fish had disappeared, and we were alone again in the ocean, the rock of the tide pulling back, the muscular grunt of the manatee's back pulling us both through the water in strong, even strokes.

The truth is, for a long time I felt nothing, was nothing. Lolly Emmerson, who ever she was or is, ceased. That is something I have not told people. The truth is, for a time I was nothing but the water, and the water entered me, filled my ears and eyes and I closed off my senses and became nothing but foam and hope. I did not have an identity separate from the manatee. I could not risk being other than an animal.

Then I smelled land.

It came across the wave tops like a brown scent of rolls and butter. I lifted slightly from the manatee and tried to capture the direction, but I could not see above the movement of the waves. I tried to triangulate, to make observations, but that no longer felt possible. I followed my nose. With each thrust of the manatee's fins the scent of land grew deeper and drier. Mangrove, soil, bark, seed, rot, fungi, leaf, twig, root. I felt the land as an animal feels its element: I opened my nostrils wider and the chill that knitted my muscles tighter felt momentarily calmer. The moon passed behind a cloud and when it returned to the open sky I saw dark trees and underbrush fifty yards on my left, the tree line a stiff brush of vegetation that appeared darker than the sea, and more watchful.

Now, I told myself.

That part of my mind that still believed I controlled something insisted I swim for it. Fifty yards, that was all. Forty yards and I would have sand under my feet. As tired as I was, as cold as I felt, I knew I could swim to shore. I had no idea what the shoreline held for me, and I did not trust it immediately, but that seemed to be the prudent thing to do. Get to land. Then figure it out.

I didn't let go of the manatee, though.

I didn't let go because I was afraid.

I was afraid to be alone in the sea again, and I was afraid of the alligators that sometimes rested on mangrove keys, and I did not want to put my feet down in a black hummock of soil and water and swim to the bushes of a forbidding, isolated island. If I made it, I would be on an island or key by myself, perhaps miles away from anywhere. I could not know absolutely if the trees rested on true soil. In the Everglades, things grew as nowhere else. Trees rose with moss riding on their backs, and vines twisted around everything like wild plumes of DNA, and I knew that if I made it, only to see the manatee swim away, that I would die of loneliness and fear.

In the end it didn't matter. A hundred yards farther on, the manatee banked to his left and turned toward the tree line. In two smooth paddles he glided close to shore, and when he got within yards of land, a great warm stream of water suddenly collided with us. We had reached a warm spring and the manatees, I knew, had arrived at their destination.

Some of those who doubt my story—and what do I care?—try to pin me down on the location of the warm spring. They want to know where the boat capsized, what direction I floated afterward, where the spring flowed. These people believe that by knowing directions they will understand something that escapes them now. They want a rational answer, and they want to test me. I don't know if they want to be persuaded or if they would take more pleasure in proving me a fake. Often the people who disbelieve are men, though I don't know why that is. Maybe, I've thought, the world must be a more painful place for men. But I am not a man, so I can't say.

People may ask me a million times for a million years, and I will not tell them where the manatees took me. I will not even provide landmarks, and, if you are reading closely, you will notice I have kept the details of my sailing voyage vague. I did that on purpose. I refuse to contribute to anything that can injure the manatees or give away their hiding place. They have few hiding places left, I know. I was there.

Some people have compared me to Elian Gonzalez. In

November of 1999, Elian and his mother climbed onto a 5.5-meter vessel—usually described as a canoe or a raft—for the ninety-mile trip from Cuba to Florida. Fourteen people boarded the boat; they shared two inner tubes as life rafts. The boat capsized not far into the trip and everyone went into the water. Three people survived: Nivaldo Fernandez, Arianne Horta, and Elian.

Elian's mother died. No one knows if he watched her death. He was six years old.

After Elian was saved off the coast of Fort Lauderdale, rumors started that a Santeria priest had prophesied to Fidel Castro that he would be overthrown by a child who had been saved by angels of the sea. Dolphins, according to several stories, nudged Elian back onto the inner tube when he slipped off, and they protected him from sharks. As he was saved, Elian reached upward toward an angel who, he said, floated above him.

He had no scratches on his legs; he was not particularly dehydrated; his legs had no fish bites at all; the sun had not burned his skin raw.

Later, an image of the Virgin Mary appeared in a mirror in Elian's bedroom. Another image appeared in an oil stain on a nearby bank window. A columnist in a Cuban paper in Florida wrote: "The daughter of the pharaoh took in Moses and this changed the history of the Hebrews. Moses lived to lead his people out of slavery in Egypt to the promised land of Israel, an exodus that lasted forty years—about the same as our exile from Cuba."

An artist named Alexis Bianco painted *El Niño de los Delfines*. A beam of light descending from above illuminates Elian in his inner tube, with three dolphins protecting him. In time a religious movement sprang up around Elian. People slept outside his house and asked him to bless their children.

Whether Elian's story is true or not, I can't say. But I am not Elian. I saw no angels. No light descended on me. I have never seen the image of the Virgin Mary in my bathroom mirror and I don't expect to anytime soon. Nothing about this story is miraculous except the existence of the manatees. And they were miraculous before me, and will be long after I am gone.

For a moment or two, I was not sure that the water had actually turned warmer. For an instant I believed I had lost all feeling and that I was about to die. The manatee beneath me had stopped moving forward with any discernible purpose. The shoreline now lingered just twenty feet away on either side, and I felt the manatee drifting rather than swimming. The second manatee swam up beside us, and I reached my hand over to it and rubbed its back. It did not move away or come closer. I rubbed it again. And then I felt the water on my hand and understood the temperature had changed dramatically.

A moment later the third manatee joined us, falling into the space on my right. They did not move except occasionally to drift sideways. No current seemed to push them, and I understood, as I had suspected earlier, that they had arrived at a place they had visited before. Warm water flowed directly onto their shoulders. Long afterward I learned that manatees suffered from respiratory illnesses, that they needed warm water before things like pneumonia could lock onto their lungs and kill them. Every manatee must find a warm spring from time to time, especially in winter. Manatees soaked up heat and renewed themselves. The warm springs caused the water hyacinth to grow, and the manatees loved wild hyacinth more than any other food.

It is anyone's guess how long manatees have visited the spring. But I promise it was not something they bumped into, not something they happened upon. They came for the warm water and they stopped when they found it.

I did not move for a long time. I let the warm water pour over me. Gradually, as if returning from a great distance, my body came back to me. I felt my toes slowly begin to ache, and that ache moved up my calves, then into my thighs. When the ache reached my core—my belly and back and groin—I could barely suppress a scream. I rolled slowly onto my back, so that my back drifted above the back of my manatee, and I looked up at the stars. The moon had drifted down lower to the horizon, and I wondered what time it could be. Now and then one of the manatees lifted its head and blew air from its nostrils, and they sounded like horses drowsing in a hay-filled barn. I tried to picture land, beautiful land, with rolling hills and the sun high all day long. My grandparents in upstate New York had a barn like that, with two horses and a donkey named Herbert. For a time, looking at the stars, my mind traveled there. I'm sure I slept. The warmth pushed at me and I hung in my life jacket, my heels resting on the broad back of my manatee, and I dozed and felt warm and dreamed, moving in and out of sleep as the water pushed me deeper into warmth.

Around me insects called, and now and then I heard fish jump and leave the water. Once, in the darkness, a large animal moved off to our right, and I wondered if an alligator had slid from a mudbank into the current, but I did not fear an alligator as long as I had the manatees near me. Later a heron passed above our spring, and I watched him fly with slow wingbeats, his beak shoved forward like a bowsprit. His wings took darkness and threw it up over its back.

Close to dawn a strange thing occurred. My head had fallen slowly backward in sleep and a movement of the manatee beneath me had tilted my legs higher so that my ears had submerged. Maybe the approaching sun woke me. I can't say. But my eyes opened, and for a second the entire world was silent. The stars lingered above me and the warm water bathed me, and I felt my soul drifting above. It was not a supernatural sensation at all. I had merely merged somehow with the things around me, and I felt as peaceful as I had ever felt, and twice, beneath me, I heard the manatees chirp to each other, and such sublime contentment rushed over me that I knew the entire experience had been worth this single moment. I told myself to remember, to hold this moment, because I would let the world brush it away, the business of everyday life, if I wasn't careful. Then I wondered if every moment couldn't contain these elements, if this is what the Buddhists meant by enlightenment and true consciousness. As I wondered, the sun began to lift the birds out of the trees around us, and a gull suddenly swung by, and the manatees shifted. I pulled myself forward and my feet drifted down, and I began to cry from exhaustion and beauty, and from not knowing the difference between the two.

7

A list, in no order, of things I wanted most:

1. Sherbet.
2. Water.
3. Dry wool socks.
4. Clean hair, clean body, clean underwear.
5. A rice-and-black-bean wrap from Comma, the Cuban woman who cooked off the dock at the fishing wharf. And a cold Nestea iced tea. A dark piece of chocolate for dessert.
6. The smell of wood smoke.
7. An orange from Maael's Grove.
8. A thick book with dry pages and a good light to read by, maybe in bed.
9. Chunky peanut butter on a Wheat Thin.

Worse than the people who did not believe anything about my story were the people who believed their own story and applied it to me. In their story, the one they needed, they imagined the manatees as more conscious of me than they were. They wanted the Lassie thing, the human-connected-to-dog thing. They wanted the manatees to huddle around me and roll on their backs so I could pet them.

It was different than that.

For one thing, as the sun started to fill the trees and pry the birds out of the branches, I realized I was far from being rescued. I was not Tarzan. I could not command the manatees to take me home. I did not know if they planned to stay a day, a month, or a year. I did not know where we were exactly, and I did not know what was around us. I did know that we had found some sort of warm spring, but that spring appeared to be located in a clump of undistinguishable mangroves, a spot of green no different from tens of thousands of green islands in a vast wilderness. Further, I could not kid myself about the Everglades. They were beautiful and rich, but they also hid a million different ways to die. I knew people who had been bitten by cottonmouths, by alligators, by barracuda. I knew people who had stepped on rays or lemon sharks, whose ankles had been torn by the side of a crab shell and the cut had festered and boiled with infection before antibiotics had knocked it back. Sunlight could blister you. Insects, more insects than a human could imagine, might descend and cover you at any time. And still there were sharks in the water, and ways to drown you could not anticipate until the circumstances nearly killed you.

I needed to be out of the water.

I knew that. I watched the sun slowly fill the trees. Then light bled out of the land and seeped slowly into the sea, turning the water a pale green. I turned my body on the manatee. A few minnows had collected around him, and I watched them swim close and peck, then flee as if they could not believe their daring.

Little by little, the manatees emerged from the darkness. My manatee, the largest, possessed an enormous gray head. I could not see his expression, but judging from the profiles of the other two that rested on either side of me, a dull snout centered his face. Whiskers protruded from either side of his nose, and from time to time I saw a push of water bend the whiskers and make them flex. But it was his size that startled me more than anything else. Adult manatees can grow over nine feet long and weigh more than a thousand pounds, and this one, certainly, had reached full size. His front flippers seemed undersized for the job of propelling him through the water; his paddle-shaped tail, I supposed, worked primarily as a rudder. The two manatees on either side of him looked to be younger and less mature. But their backs, when arranged side by side, stretched nearly across the small lagoon that contained the spring.

It took all my willpower to release my hold on the manatee.

Twice I lifted my body free, drifting slowly away, and twice I paddled back. I couldn't bear the thought that they might abandon me, or continue their journey elsewhere. I'm sure I was not thinking clearly. Each time I moved I felt the manatees slipping away, like a fumbled cookie that you snatch from your chest as it moves toward the floor. The same jolt of panic filled me each time I lost contact with them.

On my third try, I put my feet down next to the shore. I worried about alligators and about anything else that might linger in the sand, but nothing touched me. I stepped twice upward, climbing the short, abrupt bank, and then, with a lunge, I gained the land.

Everything began to shake. My bladder emptied. I'm not sure why, and I am embarrassed by it, but that is the truth. My weight, the gravity of being out of the water, pushed down on me. At the same time, I felt grateful to be on land, however foreign, because I did not live in the water. Immediately I felt the sun strike me, and I navigated slowly, walking nearly on all fours to avoid slipping on the mangrove roots, and stopped only when I found a square of sunlight. I sat on a large branch and turned directly into the sun. I let it climb me, just as it climbed the trees, and my skin began to warm and my hair, after a few minutes, actually felt hot to the touch. I felt what a turtle must feel, or an alligator, the greasy sun burning off my lactic acid. My exhaustion flowed into the sunlight, and I sat for a long time and tried to let the heat revive me.

I dozed. When I woke, the manatees were gone.

I stood and nearly cried out. But then my foot slipped off the mangrove roots and I felt my leg go down almost to my thigh, and I caught myself just at the last instant before I would have rammed my hips into the small hollow beneath me. I pushed up, balanced, then nearly fell again. *No, no, no, no,* I whispered. And I began to weep. Because I could not be left alone. Not after surviving the sinking. Not after traveling through the dark sea at night. In the same instant, an enormous cramp took hold of my left calf, and the muscle flexed as though it could think of no other possible use for itself, and I hit my foot on the branch, trying to get the cramp to release. It hurt. It hurt so much that my weeping turned to a dark, strange laugh, and I kept banging my toes on the mangrove branch to release the cramp long after it had relaxed. It was still early morning, just past dawn, and I knew, in my rational mind, that I needed to slow down.

Then I heard a breath. Then another. And I knew the manatees had not abandoned me.

They had moved farther up the small lagoon, and they had separated. It took me a moment to realize they were busy eating. Sometimes they went under for four or five minutes; other times they lolled on the surface, straining in green leaves past their flubbery noses. My manatee, the large one, frequently stayed down for double the time of the other two. When he surfaced, his breath exploded in a pop, and mist of spray shot out and pushed on the water in front of him. A manatee, I learned later, can replace 90 percent of its air in one breath. A human, by contrast, can replace only 10 percent.

I watched them feed. The smallest I named *Three*, the

middle *Two*, and the largest *One*. I'm not sure why, but it felt wrong to consider giving them a typical name or anything cute. No *Bunny* or *Hyacinth* or *Edgar*. I was not even sure of their sex, although One, my manatee, I thought, seemed to be a male. Two and Three were too young to distinguish their gender. They seemed like adolescents, and often they checked in with One, following him when he pushed to a new section of the lagoon to feed before branching off again on their own.

Watching them eat made me realize I was desperately hungry. I was also insanely thirsty, and that, I knew, could kill me. I needed water. In the sun and the heat, I would not survive more than a day or two without water. Likely, I would get weaker and weaker, and then I would stop moving. When you stopped moving in the Everglades, other creatures began moving for you.

With luck, I thought, it would rain. With no luck, I would be dead.

As I watched them feed, I forced myself to take a moment to mark a tree that hung over the water and use it as a fixed point. East. Then I followed the beams of sunlight and marked a second tree directly behind me. East and west. North and south obviously broke off out of that. To return to the mainland I had to travel east, dead east. North would carry me farther into the Everglades and I didn't want to go there. West would take me into open water. My best chance of rescue waited in the east. I could judge east by the sun, moon, stars, or by my trees.

Be practical, I told myself. *Use your head.*

And then I heard the helicopter.

At first I could not separate the sound of the helicopter from the thud of my heart. I cocked my head and listened more closely. Slowly the mechanical nature of the sound sliced it away from everything else. Nothing in nature makes a sound like a machine, not with such cadence, and I looked up at the sky, trying to see. Later people would say that I did not signal, that I had been content to be with the manatees in their private lagoon, but that wasn't true. I had nothing with which to signal. I had no way to draw attention to myself other than to stand and wave, which I did.

I held my breath. I'm not sure why, but I did. As crazy as it sounds, I believed that my breath, any noise at all, would send the helicopter away. I had to connect with the helicopter. I had to send out a mental tractor beam and pull its attention to me. Irrational, obviously, but no less powerful for being so. I waved, but silently.

The helicopter passed by to my west. It flew at about two hundred feet. I saw the pilot and I saw someone sitting in the passenger seat, a pair of binoculars pushed to his eyes. The person with the binoculars did not look in my direction. They seemed intent on the sea, as if they could not fathom that someone would make it clear of the bay and land on a mangrove key. I knew the currents, without the manatees, would not have carried me north. Logic told them to search for me somewhere else.

Look at me, look at me, look at me, I said just under my breath.

They didn't. The helicopter continued on a straight course to the west, then banked slightly and headed back toward the mainland. The blades bled light straight up into the air, cutting the sunlight and pushing it at my eyes.

I watched them go and I told myself not to despair. Where one helicopter went, another would follow. They would keep searching. I looked around and tried to gauge my surroundings. The next time, I calculated, I needed to have a plan in place. I could build a sign, or find an area on the small mangrove key where I could be seen from above. I needed to be rational and sure. The worst thing I could do, I understood, was merely to react. I had to antici-pate as much as was feasible. Once I saved myself in my head, the real thing would happen. Come up with a plan. Follow it. Plan some more.

Yo-ho-ho and a bottle of rum, I whispered.

For a long time I did nothing at all, but it felt okay, because I *decided* to do nothing. I decided I needed to rest and to take it slow. That was different from being depressed and lethargic. I watched the sun climb higher and saw it pass above the line of the trees. Mid-morning, maybe. Maybe still early morning. I told myself I had permission to be generously lazy until noon. After that, I had to come up with a plan.

I was still famished. And still thirsty. My head ached

from a lack of water and an abundance of sunlight and salt water. A thousand cuts and scrapes began to send messages from my legs and arms. I realized the fingernail on my right index finger had been pulled back, or pried up, and it hurt each time I forgot it and brushed it against my leg or ribs, or grabbed at something too quickly. I had no recollection of how I had nearly yanked my fingernail away, but that didn't matter. Nothing in the past mattered. I had now, and then later. That was all. Each moment extended forward. The past—what had happened with the *Mugwump*, what had happened with Nicky, what had happened yesterday, or ten years ago—was a place I couldn't afford to visit.

Around ten or so—or what I guessed was close to ten—I stood and stripped out of my clothes. They were not far from dry anyway, but I wanted them to be warm when I climbed out of the water. I kept my Chuck Taylors on and my life jacket, but I hung the rest of my clothes on branches. I thought about hanging my clothes in different spots around my small island to increase my visibility, but that, I suspected, was easier said than done. I still felt unsure about the island, what might inhabit it with me, and I did not like the idea of walking around it more than necessary. One slip and it could be over. I had to be cautious, while still being brave. I had to be smart. I left my clothes where I had taken them off, then slowly lowered myself back into the water.

It felt good. I had no thermometer, obviously, but the

spring came up well above body temperature. I swam slowly around the small lagoon, trying to locate the source of the spring. On the western edge, not too far from the bank, I found a gush of warm water that nearly blistered my skin. I backed off a little and put my head under and tried to see if I could mark it in some way, but I couldn't see anything definite. The water gurgled up through a fissure, then mixed with the usual bay water and turned comfortable. By moving forward or back, I could regulate the temperature. About five feet away from the fissure, I found, the temperature suited me perfectly.

I stayed near the hot spring for a while. I drifted and hung in my life jacket. At first, I was not conscious of Two joining me. He—or she—came slowly up behind me, and when I turned I saw his comical face staring at me. His back drifted above the surface, but he took a position to my left, as if he did not want to interfere with my rights to the warmer spot. I let my body go under and watched him. We faced each other and neither of us moved. I looked into his eyes. He turned away.

Slowly, I reached out my hand and stroked his head. It was not like stroking a dog or a cat. He did not respond in a sort of yielding, submissive way. He turned a little so that I could rub him easily, but he did not seem as tuned to human contact as a domestic animal would be. He was wild—that was the difference. I was another thing in his environment, but not necessarily a more important thing. He examined me and then slowly moved away. Whether he cared that I shared his lagoon, or wondered even remotely about me, was impossible to tell from his demeanor. I let my hand pass over his body as he drifted off. He felt like an inflatable tube, only denser. I felt muscle under his skin. His tail section contained the most muscle.

The other two did not approach me. One remained busy sifting green plants from the surface. At one point, his mouth closed on a tree branch, and he bent it down and chewed something free. The tree zipped up and shook for a second afterward, and he drifted back with the current. Three came into view from time to time, but he spent most of his day up at the narrow end of the lagoon. He probably found something he liked to eat.

The sun passed slowly up the waterway and lit each section. Birds collected in the trees and then dipped away. Watching the lagoon change and shift with the sunlight and breezes, I realized this was not paradise. Paradise, some cushy Florida beach resort, is only tempting because visitors are removed from nature. When you are stranded in the middle of nature, birds signal movements that have meaning for your survival, and the water is a hunter's ribbon. Even the sun has a purpose, and it is not to warm tourists in bikinis but to gouge and dig and throw energy into the trees and leaves and into the surface of the sea. I watched the morning pass and started to believe I was a primate, gawky and ungraceful in the water, a curious chimplike thing that depended on a big brain for survival because I had no other tools.

Rescue and survival possibilities:

1. Cut down branches or something to form letters into SOS.
2. Climb a tree and tie a piece of clothing to the top branch.
3. Be ready to swim and splash the next time a helicopter came by.
4. Build a raft. Or hang on a log or two. Make something like a surfboard.
5. Go around the entire little key and see what I could see.
6. Swim. (Not likely.)
7. Make a shelter and plan to live on the mangrove island for an indeterminate time.
8. Make a water catcher of some sort so I could catch rain.
9. Set fire. I had no matches but I wondered if I could create a lens from water. Highly improbable.
10. Look for driftwood or anything that might give me support to drift with the currents.
11. Use noise. Have pieces of wood ready to slap together. Think of other ways to make noise louder than I can achieve by shouting.
12. Make a platform in the trees so I would be out of harm's way if an alligator came onto the island. Be a monkey, in other words.
13. Take one shot at whatever plan I could come up with, and put it all on the line. No retreat.

—

At noon I decided to take action.

If an alligator ate me, I figured, so be it. I couldn't sit on a mangrove root for the rest of my life. And I could not be certain what the manatees might do. One of the few things I had ever read about survival tactics at sea suggested it was better to make decisions than to remain passive, even if the decisions proved not to be fruitful. I only had so long before hunger could kill me. If it did not rain soon or I did not discover water, then I didn't need to worry about cottonmouths and alligators. I had to explore my little key. It was pointless to make plans until I did.

I put on my clothes and retied my Chuck Taylors.

"I'll be right back," I said to the manatees.

Two blew water from his nose.

I broke off a stick from the mangrove tree and took a few minutes to strip it and shape it to fit my hand. Then I practiced jabbing. It was a well-balanced stick. I felt better having it in my hand. I made a sort of war-whoop gurgle in my throat and tried to pump myself up. *Make noise*, I thought. *Don't surprise anything.* I pounded the ground a couple of times. Snakes hear or sense vibrations. Let the gators be frightened of me. *I am woman*, I said. *Hear me roar.* Ridiculous, but it made me smile. I pounded the stick three times on the soft ground. *Abracadabra.*

I walked north first.

But I didn't walk. Not really. I stepped one step at a time, going carefully from root to root. If I fell, if my leg jammed into a crevice where the roots bowed out, I would be dead. I had no illusions about that. I stepped carefully, using the jab stick to balance myself, checking with it before I trusted a root with my weight. Twice I had to bend down and go forward on hands and knees. Spanish moss clung to everything. A half-dozen times I brushed up against it. Chiggers sometimes live in Spanish moss, so I tried to avoid contact with it. Plants ruled everything. I could not avoid scraping through the underbrush. Each time my heart stopped, fearful that I would discover something waiting for me. Once, about five minutes into my exploration, I put my hand on a spider web. The web jiggled and above me I saw six or seven more webs, each centered by a black, bulbous spider. The spiders lifted their legs on the web when I moved past. A shudder tripped in my spine and I nearly slipped trying to get past. The spiders waited, their blackness shiny in the bright light. They put their forelegs on the strands of the web, waiting like men putting a thumb to a fishing line to feel for movement.

Stay away from me, I said.

I said it aloud. I said it with force and sent my thoughts behind it. Part of me wanted to slash uncontrollably at the webs, but I refrained. Good karma. I needed all things pulling in my favor. *No bad spider gris-gris*, I told myself.

Sweat started on my skin and I had to fight the impulse to turn and head back to the manatee lagoon as fast as I could. Whenever I came to a solid piece of land or dirt, I forced myself to stand and observe. *This is my advantage*, I thought. *I can see; I can plan.* I also made sure I never went too far from the center trees. If I did happen on an alligator, I wanted to be ready to gain height quickly. Gators hissed to threaten, I knew, and sometimes they chased off people if you happened on an egg nest, but at this time of year I imagined they would be sluggish and in a sleepy state. Still, I went slowly. Twice I thought I saw snakes slide off into the underbrush, but I couldn't be sure. Given the choice of believing a quick scuttle on the ground cover was a snake or not, I decided to choose against the snake. Our mind makes our world. *Positive thoughts*, I told myself.

After fifteen minutes of laborious traveling, I found the curve of the key. That meant the small area on which I stood was tiny. Leaning out and looking, hanging on a tree branch as if it were a subway strap, I saw the western edge of the key, the green giving way to the blue sea. In other words, the disc I stood on was not much more than a tangle of mangrove roots and random vines that had come together in a roiling knot. Knowing that, I decided two things. First, I wasn't going to gain much by circumnavigating the key. Second, I stood on one of a thousand green dots, because to my north and west, from what I could see, a score of keys similar to mine stretched out toward the horizon. The manatees had brought me deep into the Everglades. And that made rescue even more complicated.

I stood for a while and forced myself to observe

everything. Not just look—observe. I made mental notes slowly, demanding that I perceive things as they were, not as I hoped them to be. I noticed, for instance, that the western edge of the key might have been less overgrown, meaning I could possibly be seen by a passing helicopter there. The manatee lagoon, by contrast, remained hidden all day long, the trees growing over in a tunnel of greenery. I decided I would spend the following day on the west edge of the key. From there, I could signal a helicopter or boat if it passed by. I could not become complacent and remain with the manatees just for company. I had to manage the odds. Whatever cards I had, I had to play them carefully and flawlessly. No mistakes.

I also observed a great bank of clouds moving my way.

My first glance at the clouds didn't register. Rain doesn't mean much under normal circumstances, and in southern Florida we had a fair amount of rain each week. Looking at the clouds, they didn't seem to amount to anything important. Then a breeze picked up, and the undersides of the mangrove trees began to flutter white, and I knew rain had started out on the western sea. A few birds squawked and a pair of brown pelicans flapped by, their usual speed doubled by the gust behind them. For an instant I felt a flicker of joy pass through me. "Water, water everywhere," I remembered from the poem we had studied in sophomore English—"The Rime of the Ancient Mariner"—"nor any drop to drink."

—

I was back with the manatees by the time the rain hit.

It came like a classic tropical storm, low to the water and serious. The sky turned gray, then grayer, and the trees began whipping back and forth. Wind made alligator skin across the water. Then rain began busting down on the trees, and I lifted my Chuck Taylor to the little funnel I hastily fashioned from leaves, and watched the water fill my sneaker.

It took no time. I felt a rush of pleasure at my ingenuity. The sneaker filled and I lifted it quickly to my lips and drank from the heel. The water tasted of green leaves and old sneakers, but I drank it as fast as I could, my throat yanking it down.

I filled another. Drank it. Another. Another. For a few minutes I drank out of gluttony, or for the joy of having my throat move and pass things to my guts. Then a strange thing happened. A song got into my head, an old song that my mother used to listen to, and I didn't know who sang it but I knew the chorus line. It went, "Build me up, Buttercup, baby, just to let me down, something, something, something, don't break my hearrtttttttt." It was a nutty song, a song my mom and I sometimes sang in the kitchen when we had late-night chores or when we felt goofy and happy, and part of it was the water and the rain, and part of it was my fatigue and desperation, but I sang it over and over as I filled my sneaker. *Build me up, Buttercup, baby ...* For a few minutes, as I kept drinking, I knew I had traveled close to something. Maybe it was simply exhaustion, or maybe loneliness, but my blood roared around my system, and my eyes opened wide, and I gobbled the water and let it spill down my chest. Rain splashed everywhere, throwing tiny geysers of mud onto my shins, and I raised the stick, primitive as a freaking cavewoman, and I pretended to stab things. Drink, stab. Stab, drink. Part of me, the clearer part, tried to get my core to calm down, but the other part, the spinal part, wanted to strip out of everything, wanted to jump in the water and fight a shark, because I was *Build Me Up, Buttercup*, and I was a cavewoman, and I lived to fight and dance and throw my head back in the rain. It didn't matter that I might be going mad. Mad felt good, felt alive, and I jabbed the mangrove tree a few times, liking the thud of power that registered in my arm.

By the time I had killed the trees, the rain had lifted. It still dripped, but the force of the wind had passed by us. I felt my inner being slowly seeping back. I knew how to become primitive, and to become deadly, and I didn't much like it, but I admired my capacity to sink to a raving, bloody thing. Kill or be killed. Animal. Not the toughest creature in the valley of the shadow of death, but not the weakest, either. I could be feared as much as fearful.

This realization didn't change me much one way or the other, but I imagined my body nodding with pleasure, the water I had consumed rushing down capillaries and veins, finding its way into my deep tissues. I realized, as I watched the rain lift and the sun gradually take its place, that I was getting better at this business of survival, and that, if I were completely honest, I had every intention of getting out alive.

8

Mr. Twitchell and Mr. Donaldson traveled to Kehler's Point and back and saw nothing to report. Mr. Donaldson stood on the bow and used his flash beam. Mr. Twitchell used his searchlight and scanned the ocean. They saw nothing at all, not even another boat, although a couple of times they mistook average flotsam for the wreckage of the *Mugwump*. They radioed their lack of findings to a friend of Mr. Twitchell's, Guy Fitzpatrick, who called Mrs. Donaldson and told her. Nothing to report. Findings negative.

My mother began sobbing when she heard the news. My mother does not cry at much, so I know she felt it in her heart. She did not ask if they were sure, if they had checked everywhere. She had begun to understand what might have happened, and she hung on the back of a chair in the Donaldsons' sunroom, her belly aching with sorrow. *St. Anthony, St. Anthony,* she whispered, *please come around. Something is lost that must be found.* Twice she asked Mrs. Donaldson if some mistake might have been made. Some error or thing they overlooked. Mrs. Donaldson answered that anything might be possible.

Nicky did not waste time. After he had heard from Mrs.

Twitchell that I was missing, he pedaled his big-tired bike to Bobo's and found the juju man eating a fried steak from a backyard grill. Bobo is a large man, well built, with a moustache that goes back into his sideburns and carries up to his hair. He is slightly bald on top, the dome of his skull like a volcano mouth in a sea of gray white. Two little kids played in a small inflatable pool nearby. When Bobo heard the news of my disappearance, he nodded and said he would do what he could, but he also informed Nicky that the ocean had a stomach, too, and that the stomach sometimes had to be fed, no matter what. He said if I had entered the ocean's belly I was beyond saving, but then he climbed out of his chair and carried his plate down toward a small canal that worked through the messy backyard. He called into his house and a young girl, maybe eleven with bony legs and hair tied in plum ribbons, came out and took his plate away. Then the girl ran back inside.

Cost you money, Bobo said to Nicky.

I'll pay, Nicky said.

Bobo regarded him. Then he went into a chicken house and returned with a hen. The hen made a noise like a spring that had never felt oil. It was a young hen, a Barred Rock, which had black-and-white feathers. Bobo tied a string around the hen's legs, checked to make sure the string would hold, then handed the chicken to Nicky. The chickens legs, Nicky said, looked as yellow as cream corn.

Come on, Bobo said.

Bobo led him down the remaining portion of a small

bank to the canal. The canal smelled like moss and stagnant water. A blue oil slick wrote slowly across the surface of the canal, inscribing the news of a leak from an outboard motor propped in a rubbish barrel upstream. Bobo told Nicky to be careful. He said to take the chicken and throw it out onto the water, then slowly reel it back in. Bobo said three alligators lived in the water, and one, the biggest, had certain powers. If the biggest followed the chicken out, I might stand a chance.

It took Nicky five throws to get the alligator to rise.

Nicky described it later. He said the alligator did not swim toward them, or show any signs of stirring the water, but simply *arrived*. It lifted slowly from the bottom like a log coming unstuck and bobbing to the surface. The chicken squawked and wailed. Nicky watched the water churn under the chicken, which sometimes went crazy with fright, and other times it seemed to give in to the water and sink, its feathers pulling it under.

Drag the chicken up, Bobo said, leaning out a little and intent, the way men get when they are fishing or expecting contact with an animal. *Don't let the gator get it in the water, man.*

What are you talking about? Nicky asked, excited and nervous and feeling bad about the hen.

Just drag it up the bank and make the gator follow.

That's what Nicky did. Nicky said that Bobo became tense, because it was the biggest gator, the spirit animal, that followed the chicken out. The gator had a head as wide as a backpack, and it had been deep down in the canal, because it had large clumps of mud sticking to its body. When it pulled its front quarters up onto land, its claws digging furrows in the mud, Bobo told Nicky to step over the gator.

Step over? Nicky asked. *You kidding me?*

Right over, Bobo said. *Do it fast and keep the chicken in front of the gator. Do it lively.*

Nicky didn't really understand, but he didn't hesitate. He stepped forward and held the chicken dangling in front of the gator's nose while, in two steps, he suddenly stood next to the reptile. The gator turned just a little at him while Nicky dabbed the chicken up and down until the gator grabbed it, crushing it in one bite. A black-and-white feather stuck to the gummy lip on the animal's right side.

Nicky stepped over the gator.

For me.

To release me from the water.

The gator slid back in the canal. Bobo called to the little girl, the one who had cleared the plate, and told her to bring rum. Standing next to the canal, Nicky and Bobo shared a drink, sloshing it down with a quick grimace. Nicky said he had trouble taking his eyes off the water, knowing a gator of that size lived right down in the canal next to Bobo's house. He said he couldn't help thinking about the kids playing in the swimming pool, and the potential danger of having three gators floating at the edge of your property. But he felt good, too, as if he had proved something to himself. He thought of the old rhyme, "Jack be nimble, Jack be quick, Jack jump over the candlestick."

Hippie chick, Bobo said about me, finishing the last of the rum. *She's got her own juju.*

9

I spent about three hours trying this:

I filled my sneaker with water, angled it toward the sun, then attempted to direct the reflection. Like a mirror. Like a rescue glass. If a helicopter went by, I wanted to be ready. I wanted to be able to direct a single beam of light from my Chuck Taylor to a pilot flying by at two hundred feet.

I couldn't do it. Not with any real accuracy. Water moves too much. The sun is too unpredictable. Light is too hard to catch.

By late afternoon, I could no longer deny the pain in my stomach that pushed at me. I needed food. I had a general sense of what I should eat: bugs, grasshoppers, maybe beetles. I detested the thought of eating other creatures, not out of queasiness but out of respect for other lives. Later, questioners would ask what I ate, waiting to catch me on an inconsistency in my philosophy, because, they figured, a vegan would cave in when it came down to survival. They weren't entirely wrong. I considered eating the insects I found nearly everywhere around me, and I made a few persuasive arguments to myself in favor of doing so, but I held off for a couple of reasons. First, I wasn't sure which insects might be safe. Some beetles, I knew, harbored serious toxins. If I became sick, game over.

And second, I did not want to ruin my *chi* with the manatees.

Call it stupid or hippie-dippy. I don't care. I did not want to eat flesh in front of the manatees. That somehow seemed an affront to the bargain we had struck. I knew—I suspected, anyway—that I would jeopardize the companionship of the manatees if I ate meat, even though I later learned that manatees sometimes ate insects that clung to vegetation. That left veggies.

To survive on veggies, and only veggies, would mean I had to eat nearly full-time. That's how horses did it, and elephants, and manatees. You had to eat constantly. Without cheese or hummus or black beans to fill in the proteins, your system had to process tons of greens.

At some point, every time you consume food, a biological equation kicks in. Eat X to gain energy Y. If eating X depletes more energy than X can provide, the equation will kill you. Cheetahs cannot chase too many antelopes before they catch one. If they fail repeatedly, they will get too weak and they will be done for. Fish need to secure proper-sized minnows or eat the equivalency in insect larvae. If you hike too long and don't feed the oven, then you will become loopy and die.

The X became picking veggies. The Y was the caloric bang I got for swallowing them.

I stripped my clothes again and climbed into the lagoon with the manatees. They had been quiet for the past half hour and I guessed they were asleep. I swam to the hot spring for a second and let it warm me. Then when I felt my body good and heated, I moved closer to the banks and dived underwater.

It was easy to see where the manatees had been eating. They had chewed down, or cleaned out, strips of grasses near the bank. I put my arms forward and tore out a few handfuls. I bobbed back up and put the grass in my mouth. It tasted like wet spinach, salty from the sea, but edible.

I dove three more times and repeated the meal. I was unsure if eating so much salt would make me more thirsty. Ultimately, I didn't care. My stomach began to fill, and whether the X equaled Y or not hardly mattered. I ate because to do otherwise meant surrender.

On my fourth eating dive, One joined me. Suddenly he appeared, enormous and gray, his body blocking my view entirely in one direction. He put his head into the grass where I had been feeding, and I heard, even underwater, the grinding and gulping of his jaws and mouth. When he lifted his face from the grass, tendrils of green wavered down on either side of his lips.

I watched him until my air ran out. When I dove back down, I rubbed my hand on his belly. I rubbed it gently at first, then harder. For a moment he continued chewing, blubbering down lawn-mower bags of greens, but when

I rubbed harder, he slowly ceased. He looked up from the food, concentrating, it seemed, on my hand, and for that moment it was no different than petting a dog. While my hand went up and down his belly, I felt him relax, and I knew, as stupid as it might have been to refrain from insects, that I had been correct not to eat flesh. If that's a weird position to take, so be it.

Two and Three swam over and I rubbed their bellies, too. Each paused, as dogs will, to listen to their own pleasure farther back in their body. When I finished rubbing their bellies as much as I could, Two bumped me with his shoulder. It was playful. I put my feet against him and shoved solidly, but not hard. Two swam off a little, pleased, and then swam in a circle and returned to his same spot. I repeated the game with Three, but Three didn't seem interested. Two, I decided, was the youngest.

Then for a minute we all three simply drifted in the warmth. It was not a spiritual moment, nothing big like that. But I experienced a certain companionship, a sense that we understood one another in genuine ways. I didn't have a Dr. Dolittle impulse or feel as though divine understanding passed among us. It was simpler than that, and more comfortable. We were not enemies. Maybe that was enough. Whatever went on in terms of predators and prey did not register here. They did not fear me nor did they entirely identify with me. More than anything else, it felt as if we were travelers at a way station, and we all knew we would go on in different directions, but for the moment we shared this space and time. A manatee bus stop. We waited for the next movement, the next transition. We all knew it would come, but the schedule was uncertain, and the sound of anything approaching still had not reached our ears.

I decided not to eat anymore for the time being. I wanted to gauge how my system stood up to the grass. For a little while, I rested on my back near the hot spring. The warmth quieted me and made me sleepy. I dozed. Twice I drifted slowly away from the heat and had to paddle my way back. I hung almost directly above the hot spring when I heard the helicopter again.

At first the sound did not make sense. My ears rested half in the water, half out, and what I heard, I thought at first, was the churning of the spring. Then the helicopter sound gained more force. I looked up and squared my body in the water. The helicopter came lower to the water this time and farther to my east. I climbed out as fast as I could, naked, and tore my right Chuck Taylor off. I hopped on one foot, nearly falling, then dunked the sneaker in the lagoon. I filled it with water and tried to send reflected beams up to the helicopter, but my timing failed and the water sloshed like liquid in a gold miner's pan. The helicopter roared closer, and I felt tears beginning, a deep, horrible sob that choked me. I tilted the water back and forth in my Chuck Taylor, feeling desperate and furious that I had not come up with a better plan than this. The water mocked me by flashing light into my eyes.

Come here, come here, come here, I whispered. *Look at me, look at me, look at me.*

The helicopter did not slow. It continued on, beating the air, passing so quickly that I felt stunned and bewildered. How could they see anything, I wondered, at that speed? Why didn't they slow down? I realized, though, that their speed seemed greater because of my own immobility. I told myself they knew what they were doing. They would keep searching for at least three days. That, I remembered from a navigation class, was standard. Afterward, they would change the search into a recovery operation, hoping to spot a cadaver to bring home to relatives.

Red sherbet in a white bowl. Cheerios with fresh milk and fruit. Crackers, Wheat Thins. A vanilla smoothie with pineapple. Flannel pajamas and a clean light. The sound of moths fluttering on the screen door at night. The smell of tar after rain. The smell of dirt after rain. The thump of a bike kickstand. The first kernels of popcorn snapping out of a popper. The sound of the last kernels and the whir of the popcorn machine. Salt and butter. Red flip-flops. Freezer fog when you reach inside for a frozen yogurt. A crescent moon and Venus on a spring night. The sound of a bird's wings when it cups them and slows down before landing. The way seagulls do everything sideways: stare, kite the air, make an angle into the water. Candles on a fall night, and pumpkins holding candles and the pumpkins singeing black and soft and the jack-o'-lantern's face melting and turning the face old no matter what.

Here's what I concluded after the helicopter passed by:

My fate rested with the manatees.

I could pretend that I could make it back myself, and maybe it was important that I kept hatching plans, but the truth was something different. Maybe, if I was lucky, I could swim to the next key. Or maybe I could rig up something on the western edge of the island that might make me more visible. But I did not have much faith in any of those options. Possibly a boat would swing by. Possibly a fisherman would come into the mangroves looking for tarpon. The mangroves, I knew, served as a nursery for millions of fish, so that did not seem so preposterous. But it would have to be luck. It would be two marbles running into each other on a Ping-Pong table.

Time factored into the equation. More time stranded on the key, more time sleeping in the hot spring, more time without decent food, more time depleting my body. Once it began to weaken, my chances of survival lessened. Game over, eventually. Then the crabs would get me, and the birds, and I would dangle for a while in the mangrove roots until the sea and small fishes picked me clean. Reality. I decided I preferred to take a chance with the manatees or any other possibility that presented itself. No cautious dithering. No equivocating. Take one run at it with all I had left and accept the consequences. The helicopter had taught me that much.

The moon came up right after the helicopter left. The sun still had enough light so you couldn't see the moon well. It arched on the eastern horizon, back over my home, back over the mainland, and I remembered Nicky had called it a ghost moon. It brought luck or misfortune, either thing. A ghost moon meant change.

I watched the moon and my eyes began to tear. The helicopter had wrung me out. I couldn't help thinking about randomness. One thing happens, then the next. Then the next. Then the next. Deep down, though, everyone knows one event doesn't necessarily lead to the next. The idea of sequence is the human mind's need to keep things tidy. If we can persuade ourselves that we understand why X occurred, then Y, we soon have an orderly universe. But when you think about it, nothing has to happen. So even the first event, the kickoff, is a random occurrence that could have easily gone another way. Every time you rode your bike to the store, something different could have occurred. A truck could have nearly killed you, or a squirrel could have jumped out of a tree and begun attacking your ears. Then a whole different sequence could have been unleashed, and your story would have changed. I realized that with no more or less effort, or chance, I could have been on a park bench with Nicky, or at home in bed, or about a million other possibilities, and I never would have guessed at this possibility, this mangrove key, this moment.

That's the kind of thing I thought about. That's what the moon brought into the sky.

I told myself not to fear the night, but it didn't help. The previous night I had been too exhausted and too grateful for my survival to be frightened of the darkness. Night is a hunting time in the Everglades.

Things that slither silently seeking satisfaction sating salty seizures of salacious succulence. That's what night brought.

I waited until the last minute of light before I slid into the water with the manatees. This time I wore my Chuck Taylors and my underwear. I also wore my life jacket. I knotted my hair back with a circle of twigs.

I drifted in the water for a while next to the hot spring. My legs dangled down and passed heat up through my body. My stomach ached with hunger. The salt water made me conscious of a thousand cuts on my skin. My forehead still bulged where I had been smacked by the boom. I understood I had grown weaker. I felt light and airy, as if my thoughts merged with the water—as if no boundary existed between my inner organs and the water pressing against my skin. Maybe I had become water and during the day I returned to land. Maybe I was becoming a mermaid.

That thought amused me for a time. Maybe, I thought, my legs would fuse and I would swim like a manatee myself. Christopher Columbus's crew had mistaken the manatees for mermaids, I knew, and the men had to be restrained from jumping overboard to pursue them. I would grow a tail, and blow air through my nose, and eat great mouthfuls of grass and vegetation, chewing with the sideways chomp of old horses.

The manatees snorted around me and stirred the water with their feeding. I put my ear underwater several times to hear them chirp and call to each other. I liked the sound. The water had turned black with the setting sun, and I needed to hear the chirps to reassure me. Twice, as ridiculous as it sounds, I tried to mimic their chirping. The noise sounded more like a strangled goat, but Two drifted past me as if I had said something intelligent. I put my hand on him. He did not stop. They were still eating, and the sunset meant little to them.

Stars slowly began poking through the trees. And the moon continued to climb the sky. A few late birds settled on the branches of the mangrove trees. I watched the moon to see if bats crossed over the surface, another omen. If you saw a bat stitch across the moon, then you would get news of something important. I did not see a bat cut across the moon, but instead, a swarm of mosquitoes suddenly lifted out of the trees and descended on me so quickly I did not understand at first what had happened. They covered the water in a cloud. I dived under the water, held my breath as long as I could, then surfaced. Immediately the mosquitoes swarmed me, landing so fast it made me wonder how they anticipated when I would rise free of the water. I ducked back under, but the life jacket made it difficult to submerge. The mosquitoes made a sound like an outboard motor heard far away on a still morning. Each time I breathed, I breathed mosquitoes. They buzzed in my ears and bit the soft flesh on my neck and forehead.

I moved back to the mangrove roots and took a handful of mud and smeared it on my neck and face. I felt like a sniper, a jungle warrior, but only for a second. The mosquitoes clogged my nose and mouth and I had to duck my face into the water to escape them. I felt a giddy madness creeping into me again. *Come and get me*, I thought. *Soup is served.* I understood that the mosquitoes had no reason to leave. I had no house to duck into, no screen to hide behind, nothing to prevent the mosquitoes from sucking as much blood as they could from my body. I could not build a smudge fire, which might have worked, or fend them away with any other human adaptation. Animal to animal. Hanging in the water, I crushed the mosquitoes against my skin, then licked my hand clean. Protein for protein. Wings for blood.

10

The Coast Guard mobilized to search for me shortly before midnight on the first night of my disappearance. A cutter with a ten-person crew followed my course on the water, then spent the rest of the night zigzagging across the bay. At four in the morning they found the *Mugwump*.

It had not sunk. It drifted low in the water, but it did not sink. The Boston Whaler manufacturers proved right about that. It had taken on too much water to tow. The captain ordered a diver over the side to check the cabin. They wanted to be sure I wasn't trapped somehow under the cuddy. The diver surfaced and shook her head. *No one there*, she reported. *No sign of life.*

The Coast Guard crew tied a number of floats to the boat, then left it to drift. In a day or two, from what I discovered, they would dynamite it so that it would submerge. As they left, they radioed the sailboat's position in a general broadcast. The *Mugwump* traveled south by southwest. Unfortunately, the *Mugwump*'s drift encouraged the rescuers to consider south and southwest the most likely direction for me to have traveled. They had no reason to suspect I had traveled north. But the manatees had taken me north, and therefore when the helicopter passed over me, the crew did not fully expect to find me. The helicopter had merely flown a pattern, and my lagoon with the manatees existed in an unlikely northern location.

If I had been able to stay on the boat, if the boom had not slapped me free of the deck, I would have been saved in short order and would have made it home for breakfast.

The helicopter flew at first light. It traveled south by southwest, circling around the location of the *Mugwump*. It made a pattern outward from the boat, searching the water for me. Although they did not inform my mother, they did not expect to find a lone swimmer who had spent all night in the water. Stranger things had happened, true, but rescue crews did not usually concentrate on the irregular. They used logic. Manatees did not enter into anyone's logic.

The helicopter stayed airborne for three hours on the first flight. It made three more searches during the course of the day. Total, the helicopter crews searched approximately nine hours in flight before they had to give up at nightfall. The crew said later they had kept up their spirits, but even searching for someone, knowing a life is on the line, becomes tedious and boring.

All boats in the area received a radio broadcast that a young girl had gone missing. It went out everywhere. The bay is well traveled, and most rescue-savvy people calculated that I would be found by a boat, probably dead and badly treated by sharks.

Some people conjectured that I had been taken by pirates. It sounds strange, I know, but pirates do exist. They don't wear three-cornered hats and stump around on wooden legs like Long John Silver, but they thrive in the Caribbean and the Gulf of Florida. Some deal drugs. Some steal. It's not unknown to have them board a boat and take things—stereos, radios, money—from the people aboard. They are rough customers with little to lose. Plenty of boaters carry shotguns to fend them off. In the pirate scenario, people imagined me kidnapped and taken as a sex slave. Or taken and killed. Some imagined that I had arranged my own disappearance. Mostly my disappearance allowed people to imagine what could have happened to them and how they would have handled it.

The local radio station mentioned my disappearance the next morning. They did not help the rescue operation in any way, shape, or form. A talk-show host named Lenny A.M. used my shipwreck to bring up the subject of whether teenagers should be allowed to pilot ships solo. If we demand teenagers have drivers' licenses, he said, why not boat licenses? Shouldn't there be a boating test? He acted as though he had hit on an entirely new idea. The dope. A few people called in, most saying they didn't see a problem with it. The host continued baiting the audience, using the search for me as an example of unnecessary expense borne by the taxpayer. And so on. My whole life, and my likely death, in other words, simply afforded him something to talk about.

He said for anyone with any information about me to call in immediately.

One caller—a nasty old woman, Nicky said later—wondered whether this wasn't some sort of trick for me to run away from home. She wondered if a boy was involved. I wanted to puke when I heard that. She said where there was smoke there was fire. That started another thread of conversation about sexual mores and young girls these days. Blah blah blah. They talked about tattoos and tramp stamps and low-riding jeans. How some girls are. It had nothing to do with me or with the *Mugwump*, but that made no difference.

For most of the other news outlets, though, I was small potatoes and barely got a mention.

The day after I went missing, my mother tried to charter Mr. Twitchell's boat, the *Molly May*. She wanted to follow my path and she offered him double his usual fee. Mr. Twitchell tried to be sympathetic, but he had a full boatload of fisher-folk booked. It was an annual trip with a copy-center staff, something they looked forward to all year, and Mr. Twitchell tried to explain as gently as he could that the search was being handled by the Coast Guard. He couldn't cover half the territory the helicopter cruised, he said, and the weather was excellent, so the helicopter was really the best hope. When he said *hope*, Mom began sobbing again, because they both knew the word meant it had come to that—hope. Mr. Twitchell had spent some time as a mountain rescue searcher when he lived in Colorado, and he knew as well as anyone that most people, in the mountains or the sea, don't survive more than forty-eight hours. After that, you usually searched for cadavers.

The suspicious old woman on the radio wasn't the only one who wondered if I had arranged my own disappearance. Two detectives from the neighboring town went to Nicky's apartment and asked him a bunch of questions. Nicky said they weren't unfriendly and they weren't friendly. They talked as flat as pry bars. Where was he? When did he last see me? Was he on my boat? Did he go with me at all? Did he have any friends who could corroborate his story?

They questioned him for a half hour. They tried to make it seem routine, Nicky said, but they pulled at anything he said to see if it would unravel. They asked if we had fought. They asked if I typically went out on the *Mugwump* alone. Did I have any other boyfriends? Did we have a sexual relationship? They asked all kinds of crazy talk, all kinds of monkey nuts.

Nicky said it was weird. He said it wasn't until they left that he actually understood they suspected him. He couldn't tell if they suspected him of murder or merely hiding away an underaged girl, but either way they didn't trust him. It made him sick to think of it. But you couldn't stop people from forming opinions or picturing things in an ugly way. That's what he learned.

A local car dealer, Frank Sampson, offered his boat for the rescue operation. He called the local news and offered it. He had a big yacht, he said, twin diesels, and he said it could run all day and night on the search. He said if a member of this community needed something, he knew this community would respond. No one took him up on it, of course, which is probably what he counted on happening. Frank Sampson was a greasy guy and he used the offer as free advertisement for his car lot. Sampson Strong. That was his dealership motto, and you couldn't turn on a TV or listen to the radio in our area without hearing two large drumbeats, then a nutty masculine voice saying: *Sampson Strong.*

A class officer at school, Martha Fipps, tried to form a phone net. A phone net is similar to a phone tree, only you are supposed to catch something or trade information if you come across it. She handed out flyers in school and the net eventually led to a guidance counselor, Ms. Wilcox, who pledged at the bottom of the flyer to handle all calls in confidentiality. The net, I guess, was supposed to help authorities track me down if someone knew something about my disappearance. Teen network, in other words. It wasn't a bad idea, except Martha Fipps and I were about as different as two humans can be while still living on the same continent. She wore her hair in a flip and ran around school putting up posters and organizing car washes, practically working as a faculty member half the time. The phone net seemed like one more activity, something for her résumé, and people who knew me chucked the paper in the trash as soon as they received it.

I love Nicky for stepping over an alligator for me. And I love my mom for trying to charter Mr. Twitchell's boat, even though she didn't have the money. My mother is a lion. She knew in her heart that I was alive.

11

I slept. I had water dreams. I had dreams of sailing and dreams of wind pocketing a spinnaker full and round as a pregnant woman. I dreamed of raspberry sherbet and tea and white mail sitting in a blue bowl. I dreamed of school and a fat poetry book I had taken from the library, and I dreamed of coffee and a cattle egret pecking at the dry dung of cows. Mosquitoes drilled in my ears and buzzed, and suddenly I was in a dentist's chair and Mrs. Williams, the hygienist, held something in her hand and inserted it slowly into my mouth, and I woke with a short shudder and then dreamed again. Dark, featureless dreams. Mosquitoes sucked blood from my hairline and made a red ribbon there. I heard the manatees snort from time to time, but it was no longer possible to distinguish what happened inside or outside my sleep. I wondered if I had eaten something horrible when I tried the manatee food, but even that thought swept away. I did not fall or rise in sleep. I remained stationary, suspended, adrift from a ship that bobbed yards away from me. Then my mother called to me from the ship, and I saw Nicky climbing the mast, and the mosquitoes dug a furrow behind my ear and began to feed without fear.

When I woke the last time, the manatees were preparing to leave. I understood it in my bones.

Call it instinct or a connection. Call it anything you like. I knew they were ready. I felt it in their movements and I heard their chirping increase. I had no idea what time it could be. Late. Three or four in the morning. But they swirled near me, restless and spooked. Something had changed in the water, or in their food, and they did not like it. Perhaps they had simply consumed everything the lagoon could produce. Given the appetites of three manatees, they could deplete an area rapidly. It was possible they moved out of hunger.

My sweatshirt and shorts dangled from the mangrove tree. I considered leaving the water to fetch them, but I didn't dare abandon the manatees. I had no idea if they would permit me to ride again, but I could not risk leaving the water and watching them swim away. That would kill me, I knew. My spirit would be crushed. So I stayed close to One, my hand touching him near his wound, his body a slow question under me.

Fifteen minutes later, they left. As simple as that. They left in unison, One following Two and Three down the narrow flow that we had navigated before. They did not speed or seem panicked. They floated slowly away from the warmth. I tried to keep compass points in my head, but the night made that impossible. The moon had left the sky, and all that remained were thunderheads and the bright white of wave chop.

I clung to One.

I did not expect to live much longer.

For just an instant I thought about releasing One and staying near the lagoon. I did not want to leave the warm spring. The spring gave me hope. I tried to arrange the calculus of leaving in a clear equation. If I left, if I depended on the manatees, I risked everything. True, they would likely stay fairly close to shore, but I could not count on that. My life was on the line. On the other hand, if I stayed in the lagoon I would die sooner than later. It would not be pretty or easy. I could starve or die from exposure. I might not be able to keep enough fresh water in my system. Even if I managed to stay alive, it would be a horrible existence. I could not imagine a week, a month, a year stranded on that small key. In time the search would end and people would stop looking for me. I would wither. If not today, then tomorrow. This was not *Robinson Crusoe*. My lagoon was not a sandy beach with a convenient array of wood with which to build a cabin. In time nature would win. Nature always won, but the odds did not usually tilt as strongly in its favor.

I closed my eyes and accepted my fate. I went with the manatees.

It took time to regain a cadence with One. He swam slowly, not at all intent. He swam almost as if he regretted leaving the lagoon as much as I did. My life jacket proved a hindrance. Each time he submerged, I strained to stay with him. My arm nearly pulled out of its shoulder socket. I could not time my breath properly, and twice I inhaled a lungful of water and coughed in racking spasms while One swam beneath me. Two and Three swam on my starboard side. The land, or what I believed was the land, remained on my port side.

The cold climbed me. It penetrated me and pulled the muscles of my arm tighter and tighter. The muscles in my fingers locked like a small garden rake, and my digits moved from cramps to a distant ache, and that pain no longer had any relevance to me. My skin turned to vinyl. The mosquito bites beaded in lumps along my scalp.

In a little while, I told myself, but I did not complete the thought.

Because I wanted to reassure myself that in a little while I could die. In a little while I could surrender. I had tried. I had done more than some would have done. In a little while, I thought, I will say good-bye to my hand. I will say good-bye to my heart and brain and the air that comes into my mouth, and then the manatees will continue and leave me like a quiet buoy, all bottom weight, and I will bob in the sea. It won't matter if my hand turned into a garden rake, I told myself, because it will be finished soon. My brain delighted in the information. I felt a dry courage fill me.

I told the manatees I loved them. I told them that I would leave soon.

I tested my hand. I let my fingers relax. I let the sea begin to swallow me. I stayed with the manatee, but I felt my soul leaving. If we have a soul, if that is what slipped from me, then it is no more substantial than thought. I had begun to end. I felt it. No panic accompanied it. I had let my hand relax and felt the water invite me to stay.

I do not know how long I stayed with One. Time meant nothing except the rise and fall of his body under me. I could not tell the direction or the speed of our travel. I did not see land nearby, although darkness might have covered it. In passing I thought of other ways to cling to One, to rope him somehow with the straps of my life jacket or to hook my heels around him, but that was impossible. That line of thought proved only a trick to give me a moment's reprieve. To survive I had to hold tight, and I was not sure I could do that. Once or twice I asked my hand to become stone or metal, but the nerves and muscles in my forearm and hand began to cramp. I switched hands back and forth, but the weight of my body continued to trail behind, pulling at the fibers of my shoulder until I thought they would snap. Then something began to burn on my cheek and I realized we had passed through the tentacles of a man-of-war. I knew that burn. I had been stung before. But this time it burned on my right cheek, and I almost welcomed the sensation because it pulled my consciousness away from my hand. I wondered absently if One felt the burn of the tentacles, or if they meant anything to him at all, then decided it didn't matter. Only my hand mattered and the sea that remained always in front of me.

The next thing I have to tell is the strangest of all. I expect no one to believe it. Even Nicky, when I told him, could not fully accept it. But this is what happened.

I heard singing. It was not like any singing I had heard on this earth. A pale, high voice began coming up from the sea. It built and trembled and gradually filled my cells. It carried with it the sound of all pleasant things: dogs drinking from bowls, and screen doors slamming, and the sound of a windshield wiper on a Tuesday afternoon in March. Crazy things. It continued to build and sweep the wave tops around me, and I did not have the sense that any one thing sang to me. It came from the manatees, but it was even older than they were. It was a song they learned before we had stepped on dry land, the siren song that they sang to Odysseus. Because manatees are sirenians, from the Latin word *Sirenia*, and they have called across the seas for centuries, and I heard them in the Gulf of Florida, perched on the back of One, and I could live to be a thousand and I will not forget the manatees singing. *I am dying, I am dying, I am dying*, I thought. And it was okay at last. I could die and I knew I would hear more of that singing if I did, and I would float beneath the waves with the great West Indian manatees, and the dugongs of India, and the extinct Steller's sea cows. All the cousins of the great sirenians would sing as

I drifted to the bottom of the ocean. And as I heard the singing move through me, I felt my body lifting and I had a vision that I could see all the sirenians in the world, all the dark spots of gentleness around the coasts of nation after nation, and they sang a song that we could no longer hear, and they sang to each other, their voices drifting over wind and stars until I could not distinguish the song from the beating of my own pulse.

At that moment the sun came up.

I had not known it was close to morning. And I had not seen the helicopter lift like a bored dragonfly from the sea behind me, the chop of its rotors slicing the siren song and mincing it with wind.

12

When the helicopter rose out of the ocean, as it seemed to me, they had actually been in flight for about ten minutes. They had left the mainland where the sun had already started up, then had traveled west with the spreading light. They had looped around near where the *Mugwump* had been discovered, then had decided to run north by northwest to check anything they might have overlooked. On more than one interview show, the pilot, Jason Plummer, said he had not been optimistic about the day's searching and he had gone north primarily because they could not think of what else to do. It was to be the last day of searching. In fact, I had become a lowered priority. They did not expect me to be found alive, and if anyone else had gone missing, the helicopter would have been directed to them.

They saw me almost immediately.

More important for the way the story spread is that the copilot, Uli Johanson, leaned out of the starboard side of the helicopter and aimed a video camera at me. They had it along so that they could film wrecks or anything else that insurance companies or police investigations might someday require. Instead of capturing a wreck, they captured the shaky image of a girl moving unnaturally through the water, three enormous shadows beneath her. The sea had just turned blue with the sun.

"We have her," Jason Plummer radioed back.

He also informed Coast Guard headquarters that they would not believe what they, the helicopter crew, were seeing. In the background you can hear Uli whoop as she held the camera on me.

A girl riding a manatee miles from where she had last been seen. Uli's voice is filled with joy. She had seen something miraculous, and she could not contain herself.

The helicopter did not come close immediately except to wave and signal that they had me. Later they explained they did not want to frighten the manatees or cause me to fall off and be left in the water. They called to the mainland and asked for advice, meanwhile circling a little and figuring how to extricate me. They signaled to their diver to get ready. The diver, a man named Jules Beele, nodded and pulled on his gear.

But news *is* like a lit fuse. It can't be stopped. It burns until no one is left to tell.

A Miami news crew had rented a Zodiac for the day in order to film a story on cruise ships jettisoning their ballast in coastal areas. Before docking, cruise ships often discharge everything into the sea, leaving a horrible cloud of pollution. From an inside informer, the news station had learned of a cruise ship arriving that morning, a ship belonging to a cruise line that routinely discharged effluents into the bay. The Zodiac crew planned to film the cruise ship doing its dirty work, then splice in interviews with the company's executive. "Gotcha journalism" it's called.

Before they even sighted the cruise ship, they were redirected to my site. Someone at their main office had monitored the Coast Guard transmission, and they had heard what the helicopter had seen. The fuse had started burning. The Zodiac paused only a moment. Once it gathered the necessary navigation information, it jumped on the throttle and began making a white line toward me.

The helicopter shifted ahead of the manatees. For the first time, I fully comprehended that I had been spotted, that my ordeal had finished, that I was going to be rescued. I tried to look up to get signals from the helicopter crew, but I did not want to release my grip on One. He had not responded to the helicopters; none of them had changed their swimming motions in the least. We continued east, and One swam with the same leisurely grace he had always demonstrated. Perhaps my fatigue had finally caught up with me, or perhaps I no longer needed so desperately to hold to One, but I found myself drifting in my thoughts. I dreamed of Marjorie Rawlings and Flag, the young deer, and I remembered her writing about smoke coming from the chimney of their small house, and it was fall, and they had food in the larder, and birds had flown overhead, and the garden had turned gray, and the air smelled of syrup and leaves turning over, and pie, all sorts of pie, cooling on a pine table.

Then things began happening too fast. The helicopter swung low to the water and I heard a loudspeaker say something, call something, but I could not understand what it said. I held fast to One. I began to think that the helicopter believed I had been abducted by the manatees, that they held me captive, and so I bent closer, ducking my head down, trying to shield One from the air wash that chattered over us. *It's okay, it's okay,* I said to them and maybe to myself. Then I saw the frogman drop out of the body of the helicopter, his splash perhaps a hundred yards in front of us and slightly to the right, and then I understood what they intended. I held on until I saw his head reappear, and a bright yellow raft suddenly exploded on the surface, and I began to weep. I began to weep as I had never wept before, and it was not for me, or for the prospect of being saved, but for the quiet animals that continued without fear toward the frogman and the raft. They trusted us. They trusted my hand on their back and my legs around them, and I bent close and placed my entire body along One's spine. I clung to him and felt his heart and the motion of his body and I whispered good-bye. I told him that I would not forget him, and I sang to him in my Indian song, making noise down in my body, because that was the only language I could use. I pressed my forehead to his enormous back and kissed him. Then I reached a hand to Two and stroked him, then Three, and then I let my fingers relax and One moved away.

Later they said the manatees had delivered me to the waiting raft. Later they said I had stood on the manatees and went through the water like a girl on a surfboard. Later they said I had control of the manatees, that I was a female Tarzan able to command the animals at will. In their talking, they missed everything.

The frogman, Jules, had to ask me three times if I was injured.

"Are you okay?" he shouted. "Do you have any injuries?"

He lifted me into the small raft. I slid over the gunwale and fell into the bottom of the raft. The helicopter chopped the air and water around us. Jules held onto the edge of the raft and looked over the small gunwale like a man peeking over a fence. He had a harness ready to work around me.

I nodded. I understood.

"Can you help me get this around you?" he shouted. "It's a harness. If we can get that buckled, we'll have you up in a jiffy."

I leaned forward. I helped him with the harness. I have no memory of how it slid over my head and shoulders, how it buckled. I became aware that Jules spoke to the helicopter through a mouthpiece. He had given them details of my condition. He told them I was conscious. He said I could withstand the lift.

When they lowered a rope he grabbed it and hooked it to a series of carabiners on my harness. "You just relax and don't fight it," he yelled. "This will take you right up. Uli will unhitch you when you get aboard. You scared of heights?"

I didn't say anything. I could not think with the sound of the helicopter.

"Okay, you ready?"

He raised his hand. The hoist began and lifted me free of the raft. I spun slowly on the rope going up toward the open bay of the helicopter. I saw a person waiting above, leaning out and guiding the rope. I looked down and saw the raft, and from the raft I let my eyes search east. I did not see the manatees. I saw nothing but sparkling water, the waves flashing like white curls of foam biting at the coast. The helicopter pushed all thought from my mind. The flow of its blades turned the sun into a bright light beyond a venetian blind.

Uli covered me with a blanket. She pulled me away from the open bay and told me to sit tight, then buckled a belt around me. She called me Lolly. For a second that seemed like the most miraculous thing that had ever occurred. *How did she know my name?* I wondered. A second later it made sense to me, but that is a measure of how slow my mind worked. I felt a sick, nervous bleating in my throat and gut. I wanted to throw up. I told Uli I might be sick and she handed me a plastic bag and said not to worry, everything was going to be all right, she just had to get Jules back onboard. We were only ten minutes from the hospital, nothing at all, just a quick flight and we would be back in no time. I threw up into the bag as she lowered the rope down to Jules. I threw up again as she began hoisting him. My vomiting triggered shivers. I had been working on survival energy, I realized, and now I felt my body collapsing.

Jules came over the transom quickly and easily. He tossed his flippers deeper into the helicopter. Uli—I learned her name later—spoke into a microphone. She sat down next to me and pulled a belt around her waist. Jules did the same on a bench at right angles to us. The helicopter rotor accelerated, and the world turned sideways as we banked for home.

If we had not banked so sharply, if our course had not brought us on a certain line at a certain moment, I would not have seen the accident. But because of the open bay door, because of how our helicopter banked, I could not miss the sight of the Zodiac stalled on the blue sea. The scene did not interest me at first, except as I might have been interested in anything that struck my eye. It meant nothing, but it is a human's curse to look. Around the scene a blank dullness lingered, a languid horror that you can see at car accidents. Something bad had happened but it wasn't clear what. The people in the boat seemed appalled in that first moment of aftermath. A man with a camera pointed it up at us. Another man leaned over the side of the Zodiac, as if trying to see what had happened. A woman waved at us, not in encouragement but in agitation. She wanted us to see what had occurred.

I saw the blood an instant later.

The blood trailed through the water, and in the end it became simply a dark faucet spewing liquid into the sea. I followed the line of it and I knew what I would see. I told myself to close my eyes, but that was impossible. The helicopter slid by and the frame of the doorway gave me a quick glimpse of the manatees. Bright red blood bubbled from the back of One, the liquid as rich and recognizable as black oil emerging from a wellhole.

13

The helicopter landed ten minutes later at Healey Hospital. A crew put me on a gurney and covered me tightly. A nurse named Mrs. Gonzalez took charge. I wanted to ask her if she remembered Elian Gonzalez, the little boy who had floated on the inner tube, but words didn't form correctly in my mouth. I'm sure I suffered from a number of things. But the main thing was that the pace at which things happened seemed too rapid. I could not think fast enough to keep up. Mrs. Gonzalez issued a dozen orders while they wheeled me inside. She continued to tuck the blankets around me as we moved. I listened, but the words drifted far from me, and they had no more consequence than a lightning storm on the horizon.

Then a doctor came to examine me, and she had gray hair and kind eyes and she called me Lolly, too. She asked how I had gotten such an unusual name, and I told her. I knew she asked simply to see if my brain worked properly, and as I answered she moved her eyes over me, checking my irises and putting her hand on my pulse. Then she listened to my chest and hammered on my reflex points.

"Do you have any injuries that you know about?" she asked when she finished.

I shook my head.

"You're a lucky girl," she said.

I nodded, although I wondered why people said someone was lucky after they had survived an accident. *Wouldn't it be luckier,* I thought, *not to have an accident at all?*

The doctor examined me a little longer, then she told me the best thing I could do would be to sleep and rest. She requested orange juice from Mrs. Gonzalez. She told me to drink plenty of liquids. I was dehydrated, but not dangerously so, and because I was young, I had a resilient constitution. She said I should have some soup when I felt up for it.

"You'll be right as rain by tomorrow," she said. "Now rest a little."

"Is my mom here?"

"She's on her way."

I closed my eyes. The world went away.

I did not allow myself to think of One. The idea of him, of his injury, was too painful and large to consider. Images of blood pouring from his back threatened to enter my mind and I fought them away. I could not bear to think of him now. Not yet. Now and then, in my heavy sleep, I pictured the lagoon, but I did not peer beneath the water. The bull shark waited under the water, not the manatees, and I turned and struggled in my dreams. The sun came up in my sleep, and waves moved against the shore, and I lingered in a dreamland, half awake, the gulls calling above and a black-bearded pirate stumping down the hallway.

When I woke, my mother was beside me. I will not report what we said to each other. That belongs to us.

She brought me a container of black bean and rice soup from Sammy's, a Cuban restaurant she knew I loved. Her eyes filled as she handed it to me. She brushed my hair back with her palm. She helped me sit up and put pillows behind me so I could eat. I lifted a spoonful of rice to my mouth and ate it slowly. It tasted better than anything I had ever eaten.

Twice as I ate, my mother began crying. I cried with her and we hugged.

Afterward my mom helped me take a shower. She walked beside me and adjusted the water temperature. Then she stood outside the shower curtain and talked to me. She told me about Mrs. Donaldson and about her husband, Joe, and about contacting Mr. Twitchell and trying to charter his boat. She told me about the Coast Guard search and about all the neighbors who had called or stopped by to see if there was anything they could do to help. She said you never knew the boundaries of your community until something like this happened, and thank goodness it had a happy ending. She said she could not imagine losing me and then she didn't speak for a while and I knew she was crying again.

I stayed in the shower a long time. She did not ask me any questions about my nights with the manatees. She did not mention them at all. From that omission, I suspected she knew about the accident and about One's injuries. My mother did not like to be the bearer of bad news. Maybe, I figured, someone had advised her to let me bring the subject up if I cared to do so. It is standard operating procedure to let someone who has been through an ordeal lead the way when it comes to recounting it.

Nicky showed up as I finished my shower. A nurse—not Mrs. Gonzalez—stuck her head in to say that a young man wanted to know if he could come in to see me. I looked at my mom. She was not a fan of Nicky's, mostly because he was older. But she squeezed my hand.

"I may have misjudged him," she said as she collected her bag and straightened the room. "He came by the house and we had a long talk, and I like him, Lolly. I do. I'll head home and let you two catch up with each other. He has real feelings for you, and I admit I was wrong about that. I've told him as much."

Nicky came in as my mom left. They hugged. That was just plain bizarre.

Whatever dreams you have in your mind about seeing someone you care about after going through something like I went through, it never quite matches it. Nicky stood a respectful distance from the bed and did not come over to hug me at first. I *knew* he wanted to, but he likely worried about my health and about some weird social convention he had in his head. I held out my hand, and that brought him closer. I pulled him down next to me and then we hugged. He began crying, which surprised me, and I told him it was okay, everything was fine. He blamed himself, though, for not staying with me that night—for going off with his friends. I told him that was crazy. Things happened, that was all. It was nobody's fault. Just an unlucky break.

After a little while, Nicky pulled a chair up to the bed and sat and talked with me. He told me the entire story of Bobo and stepping over the alligator. He said all the fishermen had been looking out for me, checking different routes to cover the bay, and they had been worried, but they hadn't counted me out. They knew I was pretty rugged and independent. They said a nonnative wouldn't have stood a chance, but a Florida hippie chick, that was a different story. I knew Nicky told the story to try to keep things light. Someone had instructed him to keep the topics neutral.

I told him about the shipwreck. I told him how the *Mugwump* had dipped down on a rogue wave and had speared itself on an underwater wreck. Nicky nodded. He wasn't much of a sailor. He liked powerboats and fishing crews. He listened and asked a few questions, and when I told him something had bumped me in the water he agreed it might have been a shark, maybe a bull. He shook his head. I realized, watching him, that he was incredibly handsome. I knew it before, but I saw it fresh again in that moment.

"Is he dead?" I asked after a little while when we had both paused.

"Who?" he said, forming a strange expression that I could tell he had thought up beforehand to have ready in case he needed it.

"The manatee. The one that was struck by the Zodiac."

I watched his face weighing his options. He knew exactly what I asked about. Someone had probably told him to avoid any discussion of the topic. Maybe it wasn't fair to put him in that position, but I needed to know and he was the best person to ask.

"Don't worry about all that stuff right now, Lolly. You just need to rest and get well."

"I'm fine," I said. "There's nothing wrong with me physically except a little sunburn."

"You're dehydrated."

"I'm fine. Tell me, Nicky."

He looked out the window. He looked back at me and he cocked his head. He started to speak once, stopped, then started again. I knew he searched for the right way to tell it, and I also knew there probably wasn't a right way.

"No one knows," he said finally. "He disappeared before anyone could do anything. They called the Manatee Rescue League, but they don't have a ton of money or anything. Mostly they're volunteers. They do fund-raisers and things like that. Sometimes schools adopt a manatee through them. They can do something only if a manatee comes right into shore, and everyone gets behind the operation. They don't have boats to go grab manatees. All that equipment, I mean."

"How bad was he injured?"

Nicky shrugged. It wasn't a shrug to say he didn't care. He simply didn't know where to go with the conversation.

"He saved my life," I said. "I would have been dead without him."

Nicky nodded.

"I need to find him," I said.

He nodded again.

The first inkling that I had hit the news outlets came when an orderly dropped off breakfast the next morning. The orderly was a tall, skinny black man named Orenthal whose hair had turned to a cap of frost. He moved incredibly slow, like a blue heron wading a marsh. He took his time with everything, and twice he readjusted the tray table and the back of my bed to get the proper relationship. I wondered how long it took him to dish out breakfast for a floor of patients. Eventually he put a tray on the tray table and nodded at the television perched in the corner of the room.

"You were on this morning," he said. "First thing."

"I was?"

He nodded. He reached into the bedside stand and fished out a remote control. He flicked it on and turned to watch with me as if we had known each other for years. As strange as the circumstances might have been, I liked him for the way he approached things. When he had on what he considered an appropriate channel, he finished fixing my plate. Oatmeal, juice, water, melon, oranges. He placed the oatmeal dish cover on his dolly and it made no sound whatsoever.

We watched until a commercial break. He slowly shook his head.

"You keep watching and you'll see. You're big news."

I thanked him for the food. He slowly wheeled the dolly out, his head bobbing forward in his bird walk. As soon as he left, I turned the television off. I don't like television to begin with, but I also couldn't bear the possibility that they would show One. Besides, I imagined Orenthal might have mistaken a local television feed for a big deal. It never occurred to me that anyone beyond some local Florida channels might be interested in my story.

I ate everything on my plate. Hospital food or not, I rank it as one of the top five meals of my life so far.

My mom arrived as I finished and I knew at first glance that something big had happened. I love my mom—and love her all the more for the way she stood for me when I appeared lost at sea—but she is a sucker for certain elements of American life. She just is. Once upon a time she wanted to act in the movies, so when major networks had called her first thing in the morning, she had flipped.

"You will not believe what's happening," she said as

she closed the door behind her. Her face looked flushed and bright, and she looked younger by about five years. She wore flip-flops and a jean skirt with a sleeveless white top. She came to the bed and kissed me, then sat down. Then she stood again and paced a little. It would have been funny if she hadn't been so into it. She hadn't always gotten the best deal out of life, so I couldn't blame her for feeling pretty good that maybe her chance had come into view. She had also been on an emotional jilt-a-wig, thinking one minute her daughter had died, the next she had been saved, and finally, that her daughter's survival story was making her famous. It was no wonder she acted a little kooky.

"People started calling last night as soon as the video played," she said.

"What video?"

"The one with you and the manatee."

"There were three manatees," I said. "They all stayed with me."

"Lolly, honey, the video is unbelievable. You look like a mythic goddess coming out of the water. They broadcasted it this morning on the *Today* show. They want you in New York as soon as you are up for it."

"What are you talking about?" I asked. I heard it but it didn't make sense.

"The *Today* show. And the *Regis* show. Everyone wants you on to discuss your story."

"You're kidding me, right?"

"I'm not kidding you. It's the most incredible thing you've ever seen."

I am not immune to flattery—probably no one is—so I won't pretend that the interest wasn't thrilling. It was. A small inner glow began burning, and it was all ego, all self-satisfaction, that I had done something important. Add to that the idea that someone had noticed my little adventure, a lot of people, maybe, and I felt my head growing. Most of life, I think, is trying to bring home a shiny picture for your mom's refrigerator, and overnight I had nailed a truly big piece of artwork on the old Frigidaire. So, okay, I was psyched a little about that.

Another part of me, though, understood that I hadn't really done anything special. Circumstances had combined in a curious way, and I had done the only thing I could have done at each juncture. I had made one decision at a time, and it had worked, but it could as easily have failed. If things had gone a shade differently, I would have ended up dead and my reputation would have been the stupid chick who had taken her sailboat out and capsized and died.

Mom insisted on turning on the television. She flicked it on, looked at her watch, then pushed the channel changer. She sat in the chair by the bed. We watched a few minutes of commentary about a football player who had been caught for using steroids, another piece on shopping for purses on the street, and then, on the fade-out to commercial, a glimpse of me riding through the water. A female voice-over said, *A Florida girl survives two days in the Everglades by riding a manatee to safety. We'll be right back to see the full story after station identification.*

Or something like that.

"See!" Mom said and grabbed my hand.

"Turn it off, please," I said.

"You're kidding! Lolly, you're famous! You're the main story on about a dozen stations."

"Mom, please, turn it off."

She did. Reluctantly. Then, because she's Mom, and because she is kind, she understood. She lifted out of the chair and hugged me. She kissed my cheek.

"We'll do things your way," she said. "It's your story and yours to do with what you want."

I nodded.

"Nicky told me that you asked about the manatee. The accident," Mom said.

I nodded.

"I'm sorry about that," she said, "as sorry as I could be about anything on this earth."

I nodded again.

"I'm proud of you," she said. "I'm proud of who you are and what you've become. Not just this thing with the manatees, but everything. Everything about you."

We hugged again. Then we both squared our shoulders, and that was that.

14

I won't describe the trip to New York and the appearances on the different shows. That might be another story, but it's not the one I'm interested in telling. I eventually saw the clip that Uli shot from the helicopter, and I saw myself riding on One's back. I did not resemble a "mythical goddess," I promise, although, when I was being fair, I could see why people thought it was a compelling story. It looked pretty cool. Here came this girl floating along the surface and three large animals swam beneath her. Then I seemed to stand and I appeared to be surfing on the animals' backs, and, yes, I could see what my mom meant and why the story had caught fire. It just didn't mean as much to me as it did to other people. Not in the sense that they thought about it.

On the trip to New York we met with an agent and he put together a deal with a book publisher. Two movie companies tried to option the story, and a pretty famous director, who was "down on his luck and was thinking of new projects," called and talked to me. Eventually the agent held an auction and the highest bidder, a film company you'd recognize, paid a good deal of money for the rights to my story. A Hollywood star—you've heard her name and know her from television—signed on as the potential lead in the film. She will be me, I guess, if the movie ever comes to fruition. It's all too weird. Then the book people and the movie people got together and they talked about merchandizing and coordinating a campaign across America, and they even talked about manatee dolls with a little girl riding on one, and maybe a promotional toy at fast-food restaurants. Crazy stuff.

In about two weeks it all died down. The film, if it is made, might spark interest again somewhere down the road, but America always needs another story. The story of a boy caught in a sewer pipe underneath a Missouri community pushed me from the front page once and for all. After that, I stopped paying attention.

One especially nice thing happened, though. Boston Whaler, the company that manufactured the *Mugwump*, gave me a new sailboat. They didn't even ask for anything special in terms of endorsements. I didn't have to say, *Gee, Boston Whalers are the greatest* on a commercial or something dopey like that. The company mentioned that they might ask me to speak at a corporate conference, but even that never happened. I guess if the movie is ever made, they want to be sure a Boston Whaler is smack dab in the middle of the action. The president of the company sent a nice card with the delivery. He wrote, "From one sailor to another." Then he quoted the Water Rat from *The Wind in the Willows*: "There is nothing, absolute nothing, half so much worth doing as simply messing about in boats. ... In or out of 'em, doesn't matter." I wrote the president back and told him I agreed.

I moored the boat at the Donaldsons', right where the old *Mugwump* had been docked. I thought a long time about a name to give it. My mom and a couple of other people wanted to call her the *Manatee*, or some other hokey thing, but I vetoed those names. I thought of *One*, or *Two*, or *Three*, or all of them, and I even tried a few anagrams with their names, coming up with combinations that went like *Twoneee*. But that was ridiculous. I finally named the boat *Bob*. That was ridiculous, too, and a male's name to boot, but after saying it awhile, it sort of fit. Nicky painted the name in black letters on the bow for me.

For most of Christmas break I lived on the boat and watched the sun move farther north. I listened to the ocean and to the birds and I sketched. And whenever I had free time, I searched for One.

I won't pretend searching was easy. And I won't pretend I searched more than I did, because school started up after Thanksgiving and I was busy with that. Besides, realistically I didn't expect to find him and I wasn't sure he was still alive. Without Nicky, I wouldn't have searched at all, because I found I was afraid of the water, and of sailing, and especially of being by myself in a boat away from the dock. I was okay as long as I was moored to the dock, but I did not trust myself to be out of sight of land.

I had nightmares frequently, and often they included the bull shark, the dark hooded nose bumping me in the early evening, the boat skewered by the waste metal, the shark gliding past and stropping its body against my leg. Sometimes I dreamed of countless swarms of mosquitoes, the insects forming a mouth inside of my mouth, a second tongue, and second pair of gums, and second roof of my mouth. When I tried to speak in my dreams, I spoke with a mosquito buzz, and my tongue crushed them, filled my mouth with blood. Horrible dreams.

I bought a boat for Nicky, and people can laugh and call me a silly girl, but I liked Nicky and I figured on being his friend all my life even if we broke up. I had the money; he needed a boat; I bought it. If that seems like a stupid thing to do, okay, but I don't know what else money is for if not to make us happy and to help our friends.

I gave him 17,300 bucks. He bought a fishing boat from a friend of a friend of a friend. A few older guys—Nicky never had a dependable father—helped him through the transaction and looked over the boat like madmen to make sure he didn't get taken. When they gave him the go-ahead, he bought it. It was a twenty-two-foot Chris-Craft, with some sort of good engine they liked, and a range of about two hundred miles. Nicky spent every minute he had shining it and making it look good. He wanted to name it *Lolly*, after me, but I said he shouldn't change the name of a boat, and so he kept the original name: *Sally Go*.

The name seemed kind of silly, but after you said it for a while, just like with *Bob*, you couldn't remember calling it anything else.

We used the *Sally Go* to search for the manatees. I also became a little bit of an expert on sirenians and made trips to places where manatees congregated. It turned out that manatees have a dedicated following. People identified with manatees, probably because the manatees harmed no one. If you could not feel sympathy for such gentle creatures, something was probably broken inside you. So I made the rounds and checked the different places where manatees were known to visit. A couple of times I went with my mom, and whenever we looked at the animals she always got quiet and strange, as if I might have a holy vision any second. I tried to tell her that she needed to lighten up, but that was my mom and after a while it made me laugh.

I also arranged to speak to Dr. Geraldine Powers, pretty much the world's leading expert on sirenians. She works at the University of Connecticut but spends most of her time in the field, tracking manatees and studying them. She is especially interested in the parasites that live with manatees, and she has written extensively about barnacles and algae that adhere themselves to the animals. (Charles Darwin also wrote about barnacles, I found out.) She is a short woman, maybe 5 feet 2 inches, with reddish hair and a sharp, overly prominent nose. She had beautiful nails, with a French manicure, and they had been painted a pale pink that somehow made me think that her fingers were on fire. She had given a lecture—I attended, but the lecture was on oxygen consumption in aquatic mammals and I had a hard time following it—at the University of Miami. She agreed to meet me afterward at a campus coffee shop.

"So you're the famous manatee girl," she said when we sat near a window with a coffee for her and a chai tea for me. She didn't say it in a mean way or with the busybody attitude that some people exhibited. She had a comfortable way about her, as if she knew the secret behind things but didn't mind if other people tried to guess it.

I nodded. I felt more bashful with her than I had with the television people in New York.

"You know," she said, sipping her coffee, "you're not entirely a rarity. A number of accounts through history talk about people getting a ride from a manatee. Drowning sailors, mostly. And, of course, you know the references about Christopher Columbus's men thinking the manatees were mermaids."

"They must have been desperate," I said. "The manatees aren't the prettiest things."

"No doubt," she agreed and smiled. "So, tell me. You spent two days with the manatees?"

"Yes."

"And three animals together? I wouldn't be surprised if they had been looking for cows. Males sometimes do that. They are like bachelors roaming around. That's just a guess, though. We still don't know everything we would like to know about their movements. They winter down here, of course, but they travel up to North Carolina and Virginia in the summer. And Chessie, the manatee that caused such a stir when it traveled to Rhode Island some years back, well, she gave us some things to think about regarding their migrations."

"Why do you think they let people ride on them?"

She pursed her lips. Then she took a sip of coffee and decided to add sugar. She shook out two packs together, ripped the tops off, and poured them in. She stirred the coffee and looked out the window.

"It's a good question," she said. "We don't know. No one does. And maybe they don't really care one way or the other. It's that gray area that exists between animals and humans. Why does a dog save a baby from a burning house? I don't know. And dolphins have a long record of helping humans. Just the other day in Australia some life-guards went for a training swim about a hundred yards off the beach and a great white began threatening them. A school of dolphins moved in, herded the swimmers together, then patrolled until the shark went away. Now, what's the explanation for that? Was it just a schooling technique to protect their young? What was in it for the dolphins? They didn't gain anything by tangling with a great white. It's called altruism in the biological sciences."

"To advance their DNA?"

She nodded. She took a sip of coffee. Our eyes met.

"Good that you know that," she said. "That's part of E. O. Wilson's work. The mother caribou turns back to protect the baby caribou from the wolves. The mother doesn't gain anything from that behavior, so why does she risk her neck for a mere baby? Humans like to attribute it to motherly love, but it's more likely a hardwired instinct to protect the young so that the DNA can go forward. That's the whole game for living things. Going forward."

"So maybe," I asked, "the manatee thought I was a younger manatee?"

She shrugged. I admired that she didn't try to explain what she didn't know for certain.

"That's why it's a gray area," she said. "Maybe a scientific explanation exists. Maybe it doesn't. Not everything can be explained. You had an extraordinary experience, that's for certain. It's an experience only a handful of humans have had since the beginning of time. You see, I think we yearn for a connection to the animal world, but our curse is that we don't know if that yearning is just wishful imagining or if something pushes us to it. Why do we care about dogs, for instance? Why allow our emotions to get mixed up in our feelings about a simple canine? Not every culture does, of course, but many do. You have to ask what that behavior gains us as a biological entity. What's the benefit of it to us as a species? Is it possible we gained an advantage over other animals by forming alliances? If we showed up as a tribe with a pack of dogs accompanying us, were we more fearsome?"

"Do you mean that maybe the manatee once had a relationship with us like dogs do today?"

"I don't mean anything except that the jury is still out. It's an interesting area of inquiry, though. Science is about asking questions and looking for answers. But you know all that and I am coming dangerously close to lecturing."

We sat for a little while longer. I drank my tea. Then Dr. Powers looked out the window again. She became softer somehow, almost as though her work persona had slowly started to slip away. When she turned back to face me, she asked if I had any questions I needed to ask. I asked a few rudimentary questions that she answered evenly. When I finished, she asked if she might pose a question. I nodded.

"Can you tell me," she said, "what you feel happened to you?"

In all the interviews I had endured, no one had ever posed a question quite like that one. What had happened to me? Most of the other questioners concentrated on the procedural. What happened first, next, and then, and then what happened. Dr. Powers watched me closely. It had grown darker outside, but the angled light came through the window and sometimes glinted on the edge of a spoon or cup.

"I don't know," I said. "I honestly don't. I don't want to cheapen it by pretending it was something it wasn't. I don't want to make up something, just the details, I mean, and then have that become the story I tell about what happened."

"Good for you."

"But it was something," I said and suddenly I felt tears building and I wasn't sure why. "I thought I was going to die. I was certain of it. And I had a sense that he, the manatee, knew that my spirit had begun to slip away. I don't know how to explain it."

"You're doing beautifully," she said.

I paused. I started to cry. I didn't know why, exactly, but the whole experience rushed back at me. I felt it enter me, all of it, and I spoke slowly, trying to keep my emotions under control.

"At the very end, just before I was saved by the helicopter and all of that, I heard singing. It was the sweetest sound I have ever heard. I don't expect you to believe me. I'm not sure I believe it myself, except that I heard it. Every now and then, but less and less so, I hear just the barest whisper of the song again. Sometimes it's inside another sound, like the rustle of trees. I hear it, but I can never be sure. Then the next day I'll hear just a note of it inside a wave breaking on the shore. And I wonder sometimes if the sound is going on all the time, around us all every minute, and maybe we could hear it if we knew how to listen, but we don't. We don't know how."

I cried. I couldn't help it. I put my head down and stared at my lap. Dr. Powers reached across the table and took my hand. She didn't rush in to say something consoling. She held my hand and looked out the window at some pigeons eating bugs in the grass.

What she said next came almost in a whisper.

"There is no reason in the world not to believe that you heard that singing. Don't lose that."

I nodded. I kept my head down. I couldn't look up.

"Do you know," she said, and her voice brightened a little, "that scientists have never fully understood why animals play? Of course, some play is a rehearsal for adult behavior, mock fighting and all of that, but there are moments in nearly every species when the young seem to play simply for the joy of it. I am not a religious person, Lolly, but I sometimes think of that joy and I let it serve as my idea of God. After all the explanations and scientific investigations, animals still play. I've always found that reassuring. There is joy in the world. Maybe that's what you heard."

She had to leave shortly afterward. But she told me two more things. She told me that if I graduated with good grades and still harbored an interest in manatees, I should contact her. She always had a few internships and study opportunities as part of her research. She said not to forget my interest or to put it to one side. The world needed more scientists with a feeling for their subjects.

She also said One stood about a 50–50 chance of survival. I asked her point-blank. It depended, she said, on unknowable details—the depth of the propeller cut, the healing process, infection, temperature of the water, and so on. She had studied thousands of manatees with propeller scars, and some of the wounds had shocked her by their depths, yet the manatees had recovered and lived decades longer. Others had died from what seemed to be fairly modest injuries. It was impossible to know. She said it was equally plausible to imagine One alive as dead and that I should not attach my heart to one outcome over another.

15

This is the last chapter. The story goes on in a thousand directions, as stories always do, but I need to end it here. In reading this over, I realized I forgot one thing—the raspberry sherbet. After dreaming about it for so long during my time at sea, it took me a while to have it. I've wondered why I postponed it. Perhaps, I thought, the idea of sherbet still posed a connection to being lost and afraid, and I didn't want to conjure those experiences again. I like a different explanation, though. It revolved around learning how to sample things slowly, how to make small things count, so that I refused to rush pleasure if I knew it advanced toward me. Something like that.

Anyway, it was sometime after my meeting with Dr. Powers that I bought a container of Boyd's raspberry sherbet—my favorite—and brought it to my sailboat. It was evening and summer and a school of brown pelicans fished about a quarter mile out in the bay. I watched them dive-bomb the water, their bodies like hammers falling onto sheet metal, and enjoyed how the sight of their collision with the ocean came to me a second before the sound of their splash reached me.

I sat at the stern and scooped a perfect oval of sherbet into a white bowl I had brought from home. Slowly, I spooned a tiny sliver to my mouth. The flavor touched my tongue and slid quietly up into my brain. It tasted like gardens and weeds and raspberry shoots connecting with a sheep fence. I took another bite, this time bigger, and it was cool and delicious and well worth waiting for.

I have kept one part of the story back and it's this: we did not find One in our searching, but we did find my lagoon. We found it fairly soon into our searching. Nicky brought maps over one night and we spent hours examining the mangrove keys, the probable locations, the most likely areas. We also used Google Maps, which let us scan the area by satellite. We knew almost precisely where the helicopter picked me up, so that was an easy starting point. I also had a pretty good idea where I had wrecked the *Mugwump*. Nicky narrowed the search down to about a dozen spots, and we checked them all out in a single day aboard the *Sally Go*. The search, Nicky said, was good practice for him so that he could get to know the fishing areas for charters he would take out later. I knew he went for me, but that was okay. It's what friends do for each other.

We found the lagoon midmorning, not long after we started. I knew it immediately. I found my sweatshirt and shorts below the tree where I had hung them. After looking over the side to check the bottom—he didn't want to get hung up on a snag—Nicky anchored. He was very sweet.

He knew this spot meant something to me. He didn't want to interrupt anything I needed to do. He nearly tiptoed around the boat until I reached down and flicked a little water at him.

"It's okay," I told him. "I'm all right."

He nodded. Then he came over and put his arms around me. We stood quietly and looked at the lagoon.

"The hot spring is right there," I told him and pointed.

"Do you want to swim?"

"Alligators," I said. "Bull sharks."

"About the same chances of getting hit by lightning," he said. "You going to stay out of the water for the rest of your life?"

"Not yet," I told him, and he understood.

We marked the lagoon with a big circle on one of his marine maps. We bookmarked it on Google Maps. We also named it so that we could speak about it in code to each other around other people who might be nosy. We called it Sweatshirt Lagoon, after my sweatshirt, and that was a silly name but it served well enough. Nicky said he didn't know many people who fished out that way, but he imagined tarpon would school there and maybe mullet and sea bass. He also said the mangroves would move and change once a good storm hit them. They always moved, he said. They walked on their bony legs and made things confusing for fishermen and boaters. Down among the roots, the game fish hid and grew in a safe nursery, and the branches gave homes to birds.

On our ride back that first day we both swore we would never tell anyone else about Sweatshirt Lagoon. I know I have kept my word. I know Nicky has, too.

Time passed. Two years passed. With Dr. Powers's encouragement, I did better in school. I wrote her when I started looking at colleges, and she put in a word for me at the University of Connecticut. UConn accepted me early decision and offered me a small financial aid package. Dr. Powers arranged an internship for the following summer, as a scrub essentially on a research boat, but I took it immediately. She is traveling to India to study the dugong next winter, and if I prove myself, I will be going with her. I wondered, at times, if she did not give me preferential treatment because of my notoriety with the manatees, but Nicky told me not to put obstacles in my way. He said not to climb a mountain until you come to it. He reminded me that I loved sirenians, and that I would do what I could to protect them, and that knowledge, true knowledge, had to be the way to save them.

Nicky drove me to the airport and sent me away to UConn, and he told me he would be here but that he wouldn't wait. He said no one should wait for anyone, not in a way that made them live with a limp, but that he would always be open to me. He said his life would be on the fishing boats, on his *Sally Go*, that he loved the ocean too much to leave it, and that he loved me, too, and no one in the world could say how that would all work out.

We kissed a long time and then I went through the gate and left. Nicky is not the sort to e-mail and call constantly, and so I put my energy into studying, and found I had a certain capacity for learning when it came to the sciences. He sent me a photo of his first couple of fishing clients that he posted on his fishing Web site. He appeared happy and proud. The clients had caught large tarpon on streamer flies, and Nicky looked just right as he stood behind them, smiling. My roommate, a girl named Jill, thought he was gorgeous when I showed her the picture.

My mother insisted I come home for Thanksgiving and I did. She had begun dating a new guy, and she wanted me to meet him. Besides, she wanted to see me. To my surprise, the guy was okay. His name was Dan Macleroy, and he did something with computers, and he was actually kind of dull for my mother's taste. He had a partial combover, and he wore his belt too high, but he also had a dry sense of humor that saved him. After he left, my mother and I cleaned up Thanksgiving dinner and she asked how I liked him.

"He seems nice," I said, my hands rinsing glasses. "I liked him."

"He is nice," she said and took a glass from my hand. "He's extremely nice, which I am having a hard time getting used to. He is a gentleman and likes to do things I like to do. He likes to go to antique stores and that kind of thing. He's not the most exciting guy in the world, but maybe I've had enough excitement at this point."

"I like him," I said. "I really do." And I did.

"He's talking about getting married," she said. "He's mentioned it."

I stopped washing and looked at her.

"Mom? Seriously? What do you think?" I asked.

"There's no rush," she said and blushed. "It's not as if we are starting a family or anything like that. He has a son who moved to the Midwest when Dan's ex-wife went out there. But the son owns a coal-delivery service, which I guess is doing great, so he's safely on his own. No complications that way."

"I think you should do exactly what you want to do," I said. "No one else's opinion matters. And you're right. There's no rush. Just have fun, Mom."

She nodded. Then she hugged me.

It was late afternoon when I arrived at the *Sally Go*. Nicky hadn't come to dinner because he had a charter, but he promised he'd be back early. When I arrived he was busy hosing down the deck and cleaning up after the fishing party. The sun had worked freckles onto his nose somehow, and he appeared long and lean. He looked at me when I stepped onboard. We stood for a second without saying anything. Then we kissed.

We kissed like we used to kiss. We kissed like we wanted to climb through each other's ribs.

"Good to see you, too," Nicky said when we finally broke apart. He laughed.

I reached out and kissed him again. He tasted like salt and water and sun block. We kissed for a long time. He finally wedged away and reached the dock to turn off the hose. We both had to catch our breath.

"How was dinner?" he asked. "And you met Dan?"

"I did," I said.

"You like him?"

I nodded.

"I met him the other day when I ran into your mom. He's a good guy. He helped a couple of guys here with computer things, Web site stuff and all that. People say only good things about him."

"He seems to like Mom," I said. "And Mom likes him."

He finished looping the hose. Then he surprised me by lifting the bowline off the dock post. The *Sally Go* drifted a little way from its mooring. Nicky ducked into the cabin and switched on the engines. The ignition made a high, sweet sound, then the engine flooded with heavy diesel. I didn't know much about engines, but I knew he ran two twin Mercurys that had enough power to get him out of any kind of mess. He loved the engines. He told me once that he could hear the difference in the engines' voices from a half mile away.

"We're going for a ride," he yelled to me over the engine roar. "Cast off the stern line."

I did. I fended off the dock until he had the engines where he wanted them. Then, with impressive style, he eased the boat away and we did a nice half arc away from the dock. He struck a course for north. When I saw his direction, I knew where he was heading.

I stepped into his small cabin and put my hand on his back. He looked away for a second, bent to kiss me, then returned his gaze to the water. He didn't have to say anything.

It was November, almost two years exactly since I had ridden One.

"I squared it with your mother," Nicky shouted over the roar of the engines. "She put some clothes onboard for you. A sweater and some jeans. If you need something, it's in the backpack in the cabin. We have food and water. We're all set."

"This is crazy," I shouted back to him.

"It's the same time of year," he yelled, speaking slowly enough to enunciate over the Mercurys. "Even your mother knew it. This is when they migrate. A friend of mine saw three manatees up this way the other day. I've been checking the satellite photo every week. Sometimes you can see whales, but I can't be sure about manatees."

The shout came out like *man-A-teeeeees.*

I kissed him. He kissed me back, then he put his arm around me and we rode the water north. He had been checking for manatees for two years. Every day. For me. The sun sank toward the west, our left, and we watched it arcing down, a gull riding in its beam on the waves in front of us. We traveled slowly, keeping an eye out for manatees.

—

We arrived at Sweatshirt Lagoon in no time. The *Sally Go* had covered the distance in half the time required by sailing. When we reached a quarter mile from the mangroves, Nicky ladled back the engines. They rolled in a nice, healthy churn. He pushed a button on the console and the engines lifted a little, giving the *Sally Go* additional clearance. It was sexy to watch how good with the boat Nicky had become. He loved his boat and demonstrated that in the smallest actions.

We approached Sweatshirt Lagoon at absolute minimum speed. I climbed up on the bow and called out any snags, using my hand to indicate port or starboard. When we had angled into the lagoon properly, Nicky dropped two Danforth anchors. He spent a long time checking them, yanking them this way and that. When he was satisfied, he went into the cabin and came out with two cold Coronas. He handed me one, reached into his pocket for his penknife, found the blade, then popped both our tops. He clinked my bottle with his.

"Here's to long shots," he said.

"You're sweet to do this. You've been sweet about everything."

"I don't mind having you alone, either."

"Still," I said.

I took a drink of beer. It tasted cold and right. I sat on the starboard gunwale and looked at the lagoon. It had changed a little, but not much. The trees appeared older and more tangled, but that might have been a trick of memory. A few birds still flitted in and out of the branches. I tried to see the bubbles from the hot spring, but the water looked translucent. If you didn't know it was there, you would never see it.

We drank our beer and we set up a camping mattress under a mosquito net. Nicky had thought of everything. I slipped into my jeans and sweatshirt and he pulled on a fleece. When the sun went down a little lower, he ignited a Coleman lantern. It was a nice light. We had a second beer and talked. We didn't talk about manatees.

The boat rolled softly with the waves. At the exact moment the sun went into the sea, we watched for the green light. It's a legend in the tropics that if you stare at the horizon as the sun finally clicks under the sea, you may see a green line. It's rare as anything and it depends on where you are, what your angle to the sun might be, and whether atmospheric elements line up correctly. Some people say it doesn't exist, but I've talked to a few older people who claim they have seen it. In any case, we watched and nothing happened. The sun showed a bit of quivering heat as it slid into the horizon, and a tired-looking pelican crossed over the thin arch of the sun, then the night came across the sea and held the boat.

We ate Fluff and peanut butter sandwiches. The sandwiches were a joke with us that went a long way back. Nicky produced them as though they were a rare treat, but they tasted delicious. We ate them sitting on two lawn chairs Nicky had brought. We counted the stars as they came out, and we reached thirty-six before too many stepped into the sky to keep counting. We held hands and watched, and for a while we talked about navigating by the stars. Nicky knew more than I did, and he spent a while explaining an experiment he had read about involving European starlings, how scientists had put them in a starred dome and had slowly turned the stars above them. The starlings had changed course, which meant they used the stars to navigate. Then Nicky told a story about Spanish bats that flew to ten thousand feet and zoomed down on top of birds and grabbed them and plummeted with them toward the earth and ate the birds' back muscles and flesh, then released the birds' carcasses and flew off to feed again. I listened to his voice and watched the stars. A boat is a small thing in the ocean at night.

We went to bed afterward. I stayed in his arms. How we spent those moments is our business. We watched the stars a long time. A breeze came into the boat and carried the scent of land, and trees, and a thousand miles of ocean.

Nicky heard them first.

He was attuned to the *Sally Go*, and any variation in the sounds around the boat or in the water drew his attention. Later he told me he heard a breath and thought it was mine, but then he realized it came from the water. And he had a bad moment, he said, where he believed the breathing belonged to a man, a dark man and a pirate, and he lingered between sleep and wakefulness and felt his body prepare for combat. He pictured men climbing out of the mangroves, their shirts and hats smeared with moss, their cutlasses dripping vegetation. He thought, perhaps, they wanted to board us, and he lay quietly paralyzed, listening and dreaming at the same time, then slowly came awake.

"They're here," he whispered to me. He held me tight so I wouldn't jump up and risk scaring them.

"I think they're here," he said. "I heard a breath."

Slowly, he let me go. As he did, I heard them.

I pushed back the mosquito net and rolled quietly to my feet. Nicky followed. I tiptoed to the stern and then squatted down as if my silhouette, even in the darkness, might spook them. I had no notion of the time. The darkness covered the boat like a cap, and I had to strain to see where the waterline and the night divided. I listened intently, but no sound returned to me except the gentle lap of water against the boat. Mosquitoes buzzed in my ears.

"I swear I heard something," Nicky whispered faintly in my ear.

"I did, too."

Then we heard a sharp, explosive breath and I knew the manatees had returned.

I put my face in my hands and began to weep.

—

Oh, ancient, ancient creature.

Nicky put his hand on my back and waited. I wept a long time, quietly and with my shoulders breaking with shudders, but I made no sound. Little by little it became more obvious that they were present. We heard their blows, their swirling glides in the lagoon, their enormous bodies breaking the water and smoothing it. It was impossible to know how many had arrived. More than one. Their breaths came up from different angles, and twice I heard them blow nearly in unison. They repeatedly moved to the portion of the water that contained the warm spring, and I guessed they were cold from their night swim and came to rest and to feed.

"Do you want to swim with them?" Nicky whispered. "I'll go with you. I'll stay right next to you."

I shook my head. He kept his hand on my back.

Then several things happened. The sun, ever so gradually, began to turn the eastern sky pale. The water beneath us remained black, but the air changed. A bird made a single note, a twitter, then went silent again. The pulse of frogs throbbed and centered on the boat, and I felt my heart expanding and growing until I feared it would fracture my chest. As crazy as it sounds, I began to chant. I felt self-conscious in front of Nicky, but I had no choice. My heart could not be contained and if I did not chant I would explode. I chanted my native chant, no words, just voice, and then I stood and chanted to the manatees. And maybe Nicky thought I had finally gone nuts, because he stood beside me and looked at me. I was afraid to meet his eyes. Maybe what I was doing was absurd, maybe it was New Age, hippie-dippy, but the chant continued out of me as if I didn't own it, as if it came from a time past, and I called to the manatees, I wished them long life and safe waters, I wished them warmth, I wished them green sea grass and beds of hyacinth beyond imaginings. It was all in the chant somehow, and Nicky joined me. He chanted, too, and it was nutty, of course it was, but how else can humans speak to their lost kin? I closed my eyes and chanted, and Nicky's voice soared with mine, and in that final blackness of the ocean and the sea and the long-legged mangroves, I knew I would not wait until morning to look for One, because he was already here, already in my heart, and he had never left.

Afterword

I hope you enjoyed this novel, and I also hope you will be a lifelong friend to the manatee. Please remember that the main character, Lolly, rode a manatee because of her desperate circumstances. Years ago, overly friendly people surrounded manatees in shallows to pet them or teach them to roll over and have their bellies rubbed. Regrettably, this interaction with humans worked against the best interests of the manatees. By touching manatees, we risk changing their natural behavior. They may leave a warm-water spring prematurely or, perhaps worse, learn to depend on human handouts. In the worst cases, mothers are sometimes separated from babies by well-meaning manatee lovers. It is infinitely better to observe a manatee quietly from a distance. Do not splash or cause a commotion; never touch, pet, or "ride" a manatee. Manatees, like most animals, prefer to go on their way without human interference. I promise—if you have the opportunity to observe them in a place like Blue Spring State Park in Florida— that you will feel joy in their company and a deep desire to keep them swimming in our coastal waters.

A final note. I have taken license in this novel by letting Lolly hang on to a manatee by wedging her hand in an old propeller scar. I considered having her hang on to a radio leash that is sometimes attached to a manatee's hind section—the manatees are tracked this way—which would have been easier for her. But I wanted to draw attention to the manatee's propeller scars (when motorboating, we must slow down when we enter manatee waters and we must avoid manatee sanctuaries altogether), and I did not want to give anybody the notion that one could hang on to a radio tether for any reason. A manatee warden assured me it would be possible for Lolly to ride a manatee for a short while by clinging to a propeller scar.

In my imagination, Lolly loved the manatees as deeply as possible. I do, too.

—J.M.